Dr Nigel Norton felt his home on the island of Huahnara was ideal for his new wife, a widow, and her two young children. It was perfect for them romantically and also perfect for his wife's convalescence from a serious illness. But his plans do not take into account the interference of the infatuated Della, the egotistical girl next door, who along with Papa Dan and local superstition, connive to thwart his dreams.

DEVIL IN THE WIND

Gladys Greenaway

ATLANTIC LARGE PRINT
Chivers Press, Bath, England.
Curley Publishing, Inc.,
South Yarmouth, Mass., USA.

Library of Congress Cataloging-in-Publication Data

Greenaway, Gladys, 1901–
    Devil in the wind / Gladys Greenaway.
        p.   cm.—(Atlantic large print)
    ISBN 0–7927–0257–3 (lg. print)
    1. Large type books.   I. Title.
[PR6057.R365D48   1990]
823′.914—dc20   90–32004
                                                                  CIP

British Library Cataloguing in Publication Data

Greenaway, Gladys
    Devil in the wind.
    I. Title
    823′.914

    ISBN 0–7451–9810–4
    ISBN 0–7451–9822–8 pbk

This Large Print edition is published by Chivers Press, England, and
Curley Publishing, Inc, U.S.A. 1990

Published by arrangement with the author

U.K. Hardback ISBN 0 7451 9810 4
U.K. Softback ISBN 0 7451 9822 8
U.S.A. Softback ISBN 0 7927 0257 3

DEVIL IN THE WIND

CHAPTER ONE

The pungent smell of spices mingled with the sweetness of acacia blossom. Diamonds spangled the dark sky and from across the bay came the sound of a dance band, the music gentled by the distance. A night for loving, the man thought, as he stared unhappily at the sea. Man! He was little more than a boy for he had only recently had his twenty-second birthday, but men develop quickly on the island of Huahnara and Paul Lacrosse had been doing a man's job for six years. Time to get married, time to settle down and he had wanted to do that for a long time. There were several girls who would have been glad to take him as a husband but not the one he wanted, at least, not yet, and nobody could persuade Della to do anything she didn't want to do.

If only he could understand her reluctance to get married. She was willing enough to go into his arms when she was in the mood. Just two nights ago they had gone to the nook beyond the larger beach at Catta Point. There the rocks jutted precipitously over the tiny bay and he was certain no other girl would have the courage to make the short but breath-taking climb, but Della was no ordinary girl and did not seem to know the

1

meaning of fear. They swam and then lay in the shelter of the rocks and her passion had matched his own. Not for the first time. They had been lovers for months and during those brief moments when body clung to body he was a giant, sure of himself and of her, but afterwards she was so often withdrawn, belonging wholly to herself, as if the ecstasy had never been. Passion spent he longed for tenderness, clinging hands and gentle words. Della, complete mistress of herself would say they must be going.

Tonight there had been a few light kisses, a short space in which she let him hold her in his arms, and now they sat outside her home with Della two steps above him which she managed to be most of the time, either literally or figuratively. Only when she gave herself to him did he feel she was his. When it was over he was afraid of the future and too young to realise how much power over him his fears gave her.

It wasn't lack of money that made her refuse to marry him for his father paid him well and socially his family stood well in island society. He wasn't shocked that she went into his arms so eagerly for, in the tropic warmth, it often happened between young couples, but it worried him. An ardent Catholic, he hadn't wanted to experience sex outside of marriage and it nagged at his conscience when he went to confession.

2

Della was clearly miles away, and deep in his heart he was afraid her thoughts were with Nigel Norton who was due back from England in the morning. There were times when he hated Nigel and this was one of them. While he had been away from the island all had been well between himself and Della. She was made for loving and would go into his arms readily, but the mention of Nigel's name brought a different look to her eyes. A tender, dreaming expression which he could never rouse. Sometimes he told himself he imagined it, that it was only the love she felt for a man who was like a brother to her, that he was insanely jealous because she wouldn't give him the permanence of marriage yet or the joy of letting the world know they belonged to each other. Tonight, when they had paused for a little while in the shadow of the cedars on the hillside, she had turned her mouth away from his kisses and refused to nestle in his arms for more than a moment and his heart ached with loneliness.

He wanted to talk but was scared in case Della withdrew even farther into herself—or, worse, laughed at him because he said the wrong thing. She could so easily make him feel a fool in spite of the love between them—or was it love? Tonight he was full of doubts. It was the girl who broke the silence, stretching her arms wide and throwing back her head as if to embrace the starry sky.

3

'Isn't it a gorgeous night? I can't understand anyone wanting to stay away from Huahnara. And in England of all places. Cold, wet and gloomy! I hated it just as much as I hated school.'

He was right, she was thinking of Nigel and longing to see him again. It was no use pretending. Better face up to it.

'Nigel is due back tomorrow, isn't he?' Stupid to put it like that. He knew he was due back and she knew that he knew it. She didn't seem to notice anything silly in his words, she was too far away from him.

'M-m-m.' She wriggled her strong, straight back until she settled herself more comfortably against the railing. 'He says he's got a surprise for us. I wonder what it is? I wouldn't mind betting it's a new car.'

'You'll know soon enough. Are you going to the airport?'

'Of course. Uncle Robert always takes me to meet him if he's been away. When I used to come home on holiday Nigel always came to meet me.' 'Uncle Robert' was a courtesy title. The Grants and the Nortons had been next door neighbours since before Della was born.

'Would you like a drink before you go?' It was a polite gesture, no more, and Paul knew it. Della wanted to be rid of him.

'No, thanks. I'd better get along. I've got to be up early in the morning. We've a

4

shipment due. Good night, dearest. Sleep well. Remember me to Nigel.'

He strode down the garden path, his slim, athlete's body moving with natural grace, his close-cropped head held high. Della hardly noticed his going. He was just another of the boys (or men!) in her life, more singularly devoted than others.

Paul was a gentle boy with a great depth to his character and he longed, with pitiful simplicity, to be good in the best sense of the word. He wanted to live an honest, upright life within the teachings of the Church and suddenly he almost hated the girl who meant so much to him. Hated because she held him so strongly in the hollows of her slim hands. Hated because he was going against all his preconceived ideas of right and wrong, but the hate was mixed with a love which welled up in his young body and the love was much stronger. He blamed himself for having given way to temptation for he had made Della his accomplice. He hadn't the faintest idea that she was not the slightest bit concerned about right or wrong. But it would all come right, he told himself, she would marry him and then all this half life could be put behind them.

His father owned a flourishing import and export business and since he left school Paul had worked for him and enjoyed it. He admired his parents intensely, they had worked hard all their lives and home was a happy place. Unlike some of the islanders he was indifferent to the fact that he was very dark and his hair kinky, he was proud of his older brother who was a doctor and delighted that his younger brother and sister were both doing well at school. For himself he was much happier in the business than carrying on with study. He knew his parents were pleased that this was so and proud of the way he worked. As far as they were concerned the only fly in the ointment was Della. She was a good time girl and they didn't approve. They wished he would find some nice girl and get married, the sooner the better, and then he would be finished with this nonsense of trailing around after a girl who didn't care one rap about him. Paul's mind harked back to a conversation he had had with his mother only a week ago. For once she had alluded to their colour.

'Della won't marry a coloured boy, Paul. She'll marry a white man, mark my words.'

'Della's coloured herself, Mama. Her father may be white but her mother wasn't. I remember her.' He hadn't met his mother's anxious eyes.

Stella Lacrosse lifted her dark eyes heavenwards and said no more.

Della's mother stood out in Paul's memory because even as a boy of eight or nine her beauty had impressed him. It wasn't only

6

that. She was kind and gay, with a rich, laughing voice. He remembered clearly the last time he had had tea with them and the way she coaxed him to eat more than he should have done although with the best of intentions.

'Come, boy, you sure must be able to eat more than that.' She had no idea that rich cakes always upset his stomach. She smiled gently, showing gleaming teeth, her skin a golden brown and her black hair curling softly like silk. Della's skin was warm olive and her hair not so black, but she had the same delicate nose and lustrous eyes but the mouth was different. The lips were fuller but they could close in straighter, harder lines. When he got home he had been violently sick and his mother had been incensed.

'That stupid woman is so busy laughing and enjoying herself she just don't use her head. Letting you eat yourself sick!'

He had only seen her once after that. Her face had a grey look, as if she had been very ill. A week later he heard his mother say she had gone. At first he thought she was dead but Della had enlightened him with all the candour of childhood.

'My mother went away with a man and father says I must never talk about her again.'

He was horrified, not only because she had left her little daughter but because her daughter was so indifferent.

'Don't you mind?' he asked her.

Della shrugged her small shoulders. 'I've got father and Tante Marie and I can have anything I want.'

Long after that he thought about it. Della had been very young and she did have everything she wanted and perhaps her mother had not always been laughing and full of fun as when he saw her. He thought about it a great deal. His mother was sometimes very stern but had she left them he was sure his heart would have broken. Maybe Della was made of sterner stuff. But, even now, there was a deep pity in his heart for the little girl who had been deserted by her own mother. He knew nothing of what had really happened, but then, nobody did except Gordon Grant and Tante Marie.

As he went into the house his mother called, 'Is that you, Paul?' He was home and the warmth and love was a benison. Della knew none of this enveloping happiness in that cold, silent house. His heart yearned after her, all doubts slipping away for a while. She had no knowledge of the love and security that had always been his and she was afraid of marriage because of what had happened in her own home. She was unpredictable because she was uncertain of herself and life. Her passion was an outlet for a loving heart that had been denied its rights. The thought was comforting. With the simplicity of the truly devout he was sure God would understand.

★   ★   ★

Della still sat on the steps. There was nothing to go in for. She was free to dream. To dream of Nigel. It was six whole months since he went to England. On her eighteenth birthday he had sent her a gold charm bracelet and it had been on her wrist ever since, and she fingered each charm sensuously, as if by feeling them she was touching Nigel. Surely he would at last realise she was a woman and stop treating her like a child. She loved him, had loved him ever since she could remember, but in the last twelve months it had grown and grown until it seemed to swamp her whole body, until every nerve tingled with the thought of him. At times it was a seething passion, but at others gentle and loving like tonight, when there was a soft wind blowing, fanning her arms like a caress, making her think of his hands soothing her tenderly. Dear God, she thought, how I love him! The name of her maker on her lips suddenly struck her as faintly ridiculous for she was a complete pagan. When in another man's arms she would close her eyes and he was Nigel. Her body and mind were far too primitive to care about right and wrong. She wasn't immoral, just utterly amoral. That

Nigel would have been outraged at her conduct didn't bother her in the slightest—he didn't and wouldn't know! She was an individual and had every right to give her body the passion it craved. Her love for Nigel had nothing to do with it. The plane was due in at 10 a.m. Go to bed now and the morning would come more quickly.

She was surprised to find her father was in. He spent most of his evenings at the club but tonight he sat in a deep armchair, a small table drawn close, a whisky and soda untouched at his elbow.

'You're in early. I thought you'd gone to the dance at the Metro.'

'No, I didn't feel like it. Paul and I went for a walk. It's such a lovely night.'

He gave a grunt which might have meant anything. His book was all absorbing. Della went up to her room without saying good night. He probably wouldn't have heard if she had.

By the side of her bed was a coloured snapshot of Nigel taken as he walked up the beach from his swim. His slim but muscular body was lightly tanned and his wet hair looked darker than it really was, but the blue of his eyes was unmistakable. He was tall and blond and looked Scandinavian, but his mother had been a red-headed Scot and his father was as English as the Thames. They had brought him to Huahnara when he was a

10

baby and he had gone back to England until it was time for university and he had always come back to the island for his holidays. To him it was home.

The first time Della remembered him clearly was the year after her mother had gone away. He was about eighteen and she a precocious six-year-old. He was studying hard at the time but never minded having her around. His mother, too, had been wonderfully kind in those early years. She encouraged Della to wander in and out of the house, pampered and petted her as if she were her own.

It wasn't until Della reached her teens that she had altered. There had been a definite 'cooling off' on Christine Norton's part. Not that Della bothered about it for she had already discovered that she did not like her own sex nor they her. All she cared about was that Uncle Robert and Nigel were the same to her as they had always been. It wasn't in her nature to love a woman, she tolerated Christine Norton until she was sixteen, then, feeling a growing antagonism on Christine's part, Della hated her. After her death a few months later the Norton house was Della's. Robert loved to have her in and out and was always sympathetic. She wished Nigel had gone to England for this extra training while she was at school there but he was coming home at last and he wouldn't go away again—or if he did she would go with him! She put his picture under her pillow before she slept.

★ ★ ★

Della didn't see her father before he left for the office, she was far too busy debating what she should wear. She chose a slim-fitting white cotton which showed off her figure to perfection and gave her golden skin a glowing warmth. At the last minute she twisted her hair into a neat roll at the back of her head. She laughed at the sophisticated reflection that looked back at her from the long mirror.

'It would take a brave man to treat you as a kid now!' She spoke the words aloud.

'Huh! I suppose that makes you pleased with yourself!' Tante Marie had come into the room almost silently, her big, voluptuous figure moving with light, easy grace, her dark face grave, her great eyes anxious and full of pity.

'All this for Nigel Norton! Don't you know you are wasting your time? He'll never see you except as the girl next door and you with a good boy like Paul Lacrosse dancing round you! He'd marry you tomorrow and that is more than Nigel would. He'll marry a white girl, you'll see.'

'You're a fool, Tante Marie, and there's plenty of white girls as dark as I am. Besides,

12

Nigel never thinks of colour.'

'Oh, he's not prejudiced, I give you that. He wouldn't care what colour a girl was if he loved her, but I know in my bones he'll love a white woman so you'd better stop throwing yourself at him.'

'Sometimes I hate you, Tante Marie. I don't know why my father keeps you here.'

Tante Marie didn't answer but she looked at the girl carefully from the top of her shining hair to the delicately arched feet in the white sandals.

'Well, now you've looked, what do you see?' Della's rich, velvet voice was sharp.

'A girl as lovely as her mother, who looks like her but is not like her. Not one little bit.'

'That's just as well I should think. My mother was a fool and she didn't care tuppence about me.'

'You are your father's child, Della. You don't know what your mother cared about. I don't want you to count your chickens before they are hatched. Too many women do that and it only leads to misery.'

Della turned back to the glass, arranged a wisp of hair and put on her lipstick.

★　　　★　　　★

Robert Norton was drinking coffee and reading the paper. He looked up at Della and smiled.

13

'Hullo, my pet, you're looking particularly lovely this morning. Did you have a good time last night?'

'I didn't go to the dance after all. It would have been daft to waste such a lovely night.'

'Dear me!' Robert's eyes twinkled. 'Since when has a young girl thought going to a dance a waste of a lovely night. Times have changed unless she was with a very special young man!'

Della laughed and helped herself to coffee. 'I wasn't with anyone special, only Paul. We went for a walk and then I went to bed early.'

'What have you done with your hair? I'm used to seeing it round your shoulders.' He smoothed back his own snow-white hair in a quick nervous movement, first one hand and then the other.

When Nigel gets old he will look just the same, thought Della. Big but slender and his blue eyes surrounded by little laughter lines. Her own father was ageing badly. He was younger than Robert but he stooped and had a paunch and his grey hair was scanty.

'I thought it was high time Nigel treated me like a grown up instead of a child. I'm not a little girl any more.' She put her head on one side and then turned to show him the roll at the back. 'Do you like it?'

'It's very becoming, but Nigel is thirty and I expect eighteen does seem young just as at eighteen thirty seems old.'

'It may to some but not to me. I've always been old for my years.' She spoke casually and sipped her coffee, not seeing the anxious expression in the man's eyes.

'Do you think Nigel is bringing back a new car?'

'I shouldn't think so. He's scarcely used the one he has.'

'Then I wonder what the surprise is?' She smiled. 'He's marvellous at thinking up new ones.' She fingered her charm bracelet.

Robert Norton almost wished his son was not coming back yet or that he wrote more frequently and with greater clarity.

★   ★   ★

Della and Robert were at the airport before the plane landed. They watched it circle and come gently to earth. It seemed ages before she saw Nigel framed in the doorway before descending the steps and in his arms was a small child.

'There he is, Uncle Robert. Isn't it like him to be carrying a child.' She didn't notice Robert Norton's gasp. How he loves children, she thought, well, I'll see we have them, a whole brood of them! She wasn't keen on children herself, but for Nigel she didn't mind how many she had. Her hand went up in a wave but he didn't see her. She waited by Robert's side, her whole body ached with tenderness and it took all her concentration to remain quite still and seemingly unmoved. Her breasts were tight against her frock as if her heart made them swell with longing to be pressed against his strong body.

When he at last came towards them he was still carrying the child on one arm, his other was grasped by a small boy and on the other side of the boy was a woman. Della scarcely saw her, she had no eyes for anyone but Nigel. She wished he would put the child down so he could greet her properly.

'Hullo, Dad, bless you for coming.' His smile encompassed them both. 'I'm glad you've come, too, Della, love. I wanted you to be among the first to meet Mary. This is my wife and our two children, Tony and little Judith. Both decidedly tired, I'm afraid. Mary, this is my father and Della, the little girl from next door.' He gave a sudden chuckle. 'Good heavens, she isn't a little girl any more. She's a young woman! Well, well!'

Della stood quite still, her feet were lead and her heart pounding. She couldn't be hearing aright. Nigel was just the same, he gave her the kind, loving look he had always given her. Somehow she managed to smile at him. She murmured conventional greetings.

'Here you are, Dad, take your little granddaughter.' The child went to Robert sleepily.

Nigel was untroubled, contented and

16

absolutely happy. He was the world's worst letter writer but his father always understood and he and Mary would get on marvellously. He never gave a thought to Della apart from the fact that it was good to see her again, bless her heart! She'd love Mary!

'I never thought I'd manage to talk her into marrying me before I left.' He put an arm round the small woman. 'Even now I think it was Tony who did the persuading. He didn't want me to come away without him.'

Robert held the little girl and bent to kiss his daughter-in-law.

'Welcome to Huahnara, Mary, and I hope you will learn to love it as much as we do.'

'Oh, Lord, I'm forgetting myself. Here is Ann Robertson.' Nigel turned to a tall woman standing behind them. 'Ann, forgive my abominable manners! What we would have done without her I dare not think.'

It was Ann who made the situation suddenly normal. She had a gay, outgoing smile, a face that could be almost plain one minute and near lovely the next. Her green eyes twinkled with fun as she looked from Nigel to his father.

'Don't believe him. He exaggerates everything and don't expect him to come down to earth long enough to explain me! I'm Mary's first husband's sister and I looked after the children while she was in hospital, that's all.'

Robert, the two women and the children sat in the back while Della sat next to Nigel.

'My, my!' He looked at the girl by his side with loving amusement. 'How you've grown up in the last six months. Before we can look round we shall have you getting married. You know I should have sent Dad a cable or something. I didn't tell Mary I hadn't and was she mad with me when she found out. Said I shouldn't have married her until he knew all about it, in fact she wanted me to come home first and she would come later, but she had been so ill and I knew Huahnara was what she needed. Anyhow she didn't say yes until a week ago and it was all done by special licence. You'll love her, poppet, just the sort of sister you need.'

I wish the plane had crashed and everyone been killed she thought. No, no, not Nigel, just those women and the children. She laughed and turned her dark eyes to the man at her side.

'I've never wanted a sister, you know. I'm desperately selfish and would have had to learn to share!'

'Tell that to the Marines. You'd have loved it. How's your father and Tante Marie?'

'They're fine. Tante Marie approves of me less and less! She's getting a proper scold. How old are the children?'

'Judith is two and a half and Tony five. Their father was killed in a road accident

18

when Judith was a month old. I hadn't been in the hospital long when Mary was brought in with pneumonia. It was touch and go for some time. Poor kid, she'd been overworking for months and months and hardly had any resistance. She's getting stronger but even now she hasn't quite recovered.'

Della knew he hadn't the slightest idea of the thoughts going through her mind. How Tante Marie would laugh! She wished she could turn round and look at Mary. What was she like? She had been too consumed with rage to really see either of the women apart from the fact that Mary was small and Ann taller than she was herself and no longer young and very English.

At the house she refused to go in and managed the refusal with utter grace.

'Not now.' She saw Mary clearly, wondered what could have made Nigel marry her, hated her with vicious intensity and yet was amused. What a fool she must be to think she would be happy with Nigel! In spite of her thoughts her smile was as innocent as a child's. 'You must want to get unpacked and straightened out. I just want to say welcome home. May I pop in for a cup of tea this afternoon and get to know you all?'

'Of course.' Mary's smile was tired but warm. 'Nigel's told us all about you and I've been looking forward to meeting you.'

Tante Marie was waiting, the dark face

compassionate. She knew by every line of the girl's tense body that something was drastically wrong.

'Now you can have your laugh, Tante Marie! Nigel's married his white girl. Not that she is a girl. She's got two children and her sister-in-law with her. God, he must have been out of his mind. She's older than he is and downright plain. Well, go on, laugh, blast you!'

'Child, child, I don't want to laugh. My heart is aching too much. Don't look so bitter. It does no good. Can't you learn to accept?'

Suddenly the girl was in her arms, weeping with passionate fury. Only a few moments did she stay in the gentle embrace. She pulled away and walked to a small table where a blue Chinese vase glowed delicately in a shaft of sunlight. The girl picked it up and then deliberately smashed it on the floor. The first violence of her anger spent she picked up a china figure. Lace edged petticoat peeped demurely from under the blue skirt. Hands folded neatly in front and eyes downcast. Della stared at the face intently and then, taking it in both hands snapped off the head. The cold, calculating cruelty in her lovely face chilled Tante Marie's spine.

'Della, Della,' her voice was a husky whisper.

'I'm going up for a rest. Bring me some

20

coffee, Tante Marie.'

Della lay stretched on her bed with her hands behind her head. No trace was left of her weeping nor her temper. As Tante Marie brought in the coffee she smiled as if there was nothing to disturb the contentment of her world.

'Tante Marie, how did you know this would happen?'

'I don't know, child. Something told me you were not the girl he would love. Something deep inside me. I didn't want you to break your heart.'

'Me break my heart! Don't be silly!' Della's mouth hardened. 'I shan't break my heart.'

'What do you mean by that?'

'Just what I say. If a heart breaks it won't be mine. You'll know what I mean when you meet her.' Her smile held sardonic amusement.

'If you are up to mischief, Della, honey, don't do it. I know what you're like when you make up your mind to get something, but you can't go through life taking.'

'Who said I wanted to, Tante Marie? I never want to take anything from Nigel. I just want to give him everything possible.'

'Give! You don't know how to, honey, and you won't never learn.' Tante Marie was very angry or she would never have slipped from her correct English. She went out of the room with a swing of her large hips and there was

21

anger in the tilt of her head and her straight back.

Della lay on her back and stared at the ceiling. There was a deep satisfaction in the way she had snapped the head off the china figure. She smiled at the memory. Never in her life had she wanted anything without getting it by some means or other. She wasn't going to give up Nigel for that milk and water woman. She thought again of the way the head had snapped off. She flexed her fingers.

CHAPTER TWO

The Norton house was bustling with activity. One had been expected but now there were four extra to cope with. Mary was distressed and very tired. Nigel was certain he had done the right thing by coaxing her to come out straight away. Everything was right in the best of all possible worlds. Mary was not so sure.

'You just sit down and talk to Dad. Ann and I can cope with everything. Dad won't mind having us for a few days while we look around for a place of our own, will you Dad?'

'It will be a joy. This house is like a barn for one old man.'

'Not so much of the old man. Mary, just keep him amused for a bit, my sweet, and relax or I'll pack you off to bed.' He led Ann and the children up the stairs.

Robert Norton looked at his daughter-in-law reflectively. There was nothing outstanding about her. A small, almost triangular face and a mop of curly, brown hair. A wide, gentle mouth with slightly protruding teeth and the front ones overlapped just a little. Her nose was small and rather snub but her eyes were beautiful. Dark grey with a black ring to the iris and long upswept lashes. She was no beauty, but it was a face you would grow to love for it was full of character. A woman who had known both joy and sorrow and he hoped his son would bring her happiness.

'Nigel knew I wanted to talk to you.' She leant back in the chintz covered armchair and there was a hint of anxiety in her eyes. 'We did this all the wrong way and it has worried me. I didn't want you to be suddenly confronted by a whole family, but Nigel said it was better this way than a cable. He didn't want me to come out later for he thought the journey would be too much for me. I'm sorry if it was a shock.'

'A pleasant surprise, not a shock. It was high time Nigel was married and I can understand he did not want you to travel without him even with Ann to help. He'd talked about you a lot in his letters and told me how ill you had been. I read between the

23

lines and was sure he felt more than friendship towards you.'

'I refused him twice.' There was still that look of anxiety. 'It wasn't because I didn't love him, but I am older and there are the two children and I was afraid he might be mistaken in his feelings. It could have been more pity than anything.'

'My dear,' Robert was suddenly smiling, 'get that right out of your head. Nigel feels pity for every patient when they are ill but he has never wanted to marry one before! From when he was a small boy he has had a deep fund of kindness for humanity but he is not a fool. He knows enough of life to realise that no marriage could be based on that. As for the children, he's a natural father. They'd never be a trial. Age! At the moment you look like a tired child but I've never been able to think of age when it comes to women. Didn't he tell you his mother was older than I? It was something that never mattered. We are probably both men who prefer more mature women. Christine and I loved each other and that was all that mattered and our marriage was as near ideal as it could be so stop worrying.'

'Thank you for telling me. I think perhaps Nigel wanted me to hear it from you. I only hope that while we are with you the children won't drive you insane.' She gave him a sudden, radiant smile. 'They may have seemed quiet and well-behaved and they are not too bad, but Tony is a noisy little monkey as a rule and even Judith can make a rumpus.'

'I, too, am a natural father,' he chuckled. 'The only difficulty for you will be to stop me spoiling them for you. I never did appreciate children who were too well behaved. Nigel was an imp when he was small. Now, my dear, don't you think it would be a good idea if you did have half an hour's rest before lunch?'

'You're right and I'll take your advice.'

He stood up and held out his hand and she put hers in it and they went upstairs together. Leaving her with Nigel he came down to the lounge again. He should have gone to the office but he rang his managing clerk and said he would not be in till the following day but if there were any queries to give him a ring, then he settled down with his pipe. He liked his son's choice and thought she was a woman who could love deeply and loyally, but he was worried. He longed to ask them to make their home with him but there was a fear at the back of his mind that was fantastic. He had seen the expression on Della's face when she first realised Nigel was married. It had lasted only a moment but in that brief time it was like a cold hand clutching his heart and he could not get rid of it. It was strange, but in that moment it was Della who had looked older than Mary. Old with knowledge that Mary had never had, probably never would. When Nigel had first written about the woman who was fighting so gamely for her life he had sensed more than an ordinary interest. He knew his son so well. He loved Della dearly but there had been hatred in her eyes. Why had he not listened to Christine?

He lay back in his chair and closed his eyes. It took little effort on his part to picture his wife. The neat figure, the smoothly brushed but still flaming red hair. The happy smile which seldom failed him. Then came the day when she first spoke of her doubts about Della. She had been sewing, a piece of fine needlework at which she was so adept. Suddenly she dropped it on the table beside her.

'Rob, I don't think we should encourage Della in here quite so much.'

'Why ever not?'

'She's too fond of Nigel.'

'Darling, what nonsense are you talking? She's only a child.'

'She is not a child, at least, not in the sense you mean. She may be only thirteen but she is almost a woman.'

'And Nigel's twenty-five, a qualified doctor and capable of taking care of himself.'

'Is he?'

The summer slipped away and it was the first time that he and Christine had not been in complete agreement. It grieved him to see the change in her manner to the girl. In the autumn the problem had been solved for a time. Gordon Grant had decided his daughter must go to boarding school in England. She had gone without a fuss and Robert had been surprised. It was not like Della to submit so easily to something he was sure she did not want. But she came home at Christmas and for the summer holidays. Christine had done her best to hide her changed feelings, but he knew that she was relieved that when Della was home Nigel spent as much time as ever at the hospital. When she was sixteen she came home for good. It was unexpected and no reason was given, but Tante Marie dropped a hint to Christine that she had been a problem.

It was then that Christine became openly hostile. Only a couple of months later she had caught influenza. An ordinary cold at first but it was so like her to ignore it. Suddenly she was desperately ill for the first time in her life. For a few days she fought gamely and then her heart gave out. Della had wept and wept and he had been touched by her grief. He was sure that for once in her life Christine had misjudged someone. Nigel was the big brother Della had never had. If only Christine had understood that and how much the girl loved her.

When Nigel had gone to England she had laughed and accused him of playing a dirty trick on her.

'Why on earth couldn't you have had this time in England while I was at school? It would have been so much fun if you could have taken me out to tea at half term. I used to be green with envy of all the girls who had big brothers.'

So that was all he meant. After a little while Robert wasn't so sure. She would come over to the house holding a letter from Nigel.

'He's about the worst letter writer I know. He writes a couple of pages and says just about nothing. He misses the sunshine and the swimming and he's working like stink. Not a word about anything else.' She would smile ruefully.

'He's terribly enthusiastic about the hospital and all the new techniques and wishes we could make a lot of improvements here.'

Clearly Nigel had told her nothing about Mary Robertson and her fight for life. Why? Was it because she was so important to him? He could mention her to his father but no one else. Now he knew that was the reason. He gave himself a mental shake. Brooding over something that probably was only his imagination. Della was such a beautiful girl there were bound to be other men. If only he had not seen that fleeting expression on her face he would not have given the matter a second thought. In the afternoon his doubts

28

fled. Della came over laden with toys from her own childhood. Some of them were almost new. The children were entranced.

'Goodness knows why I kept them. They've been stowed away for years!' Her hair was round her shoulders again and she looked no more than a child herself. 'I was a thoroughly spoiled brat and my father gave me anything I asked for. Once I had them I would play with them for a while and then put them away. At least I didn't break them. There's a tricycle and a two-wheeler over in the garage they can have.'

'It's very kind of you but don't heap too much on them or they'll be overwhelmed.' Mary was looking at her with a puzzled expression which hid a vague anxiety. She couldn't have explained even to herself why but there was something about the girl that filled her with disquiet. Nigel had been so casual when he spoke of her, had said nothing of her fascinating beauty. 'Are you sure you don't want to keep them? You look young enough to play with them yourself.'

'I'll play with the children if they'll let me.' Della gave a quick smile at Nigel and Mary wondered if she imagined that air of possession. 'Nigel can invent the most wonderful games.'

He put an affectionate arm round her shoulders. 'Della's right. She was a spoiled brat but a very nice and generous one.' He gave her a light squeeze. 'Don't you dare spoil our pair. They may not turn out like you have.'

Robert glanced at Ann. There was something in the expression on her face that reminded him of the look Christine had often given Della. No, he must not allow himself to be influenced. In many ways Della was an uninhibited child. Half an hour later they heard shouts of laughter coming from the garden. The children were obviously having the time of their lives and Della was a child with them.

Mary was a changed woman after her rest. Her face was rose-flushed and years had slipped off. A few months in Huahnara would work wonders. Ann looked at her sister-in-law and offered up a silent prayer for her happiness. The love she felt for her went very deep. Mary had given her quiet, retiring brother such a wealth of happiness and she had been so generous to her, drawing her into their charmed circle and making her feel wanted. When Barry had been killed she had felt more grief for Mary than for herself although she had adored her brother. When Nigel came into their lives she had been thankful and when he asked her to come to Huahnara with them she had accepted on one condition. That she stayed with them until Mary was quite strong and then be allowed to take a job or return to England. Nigel said that once she was on the island she wouldn't want to leave it, but there was plenty of time to think about that for Mary still needed a great deal of care. If you didn't keep your eye on her she would do too much. She heard Della's rich, musical laugh ring out. Why had she taken such a dislike to the girl? Was it jealousy because she was young and damnably beautiful? Or did she see a threat to Mary's happiness in the way she looked at Nigel? Either way she was being a bit dotty. If ever a man loved a woman Nigel did Mary.

★   ★   ★

Huahnara lay like a crouching monster in the blue sea. York City, the head and the capital, was joined to the body by a thick, short neck. At one time it had been a fortress for it lay high with rocky cliffs impossible to scale. Some of the old wall still remained on the perimeter but on two occasions fire had swept through the wooden buildings of the old city and now there was a new and modern one. The Administrative offices were the pride of Huahnara. Robert had his office there but said it could have been built anywhere and would have made no impression on anyone. The main seaport was Port Roy on the southern shoulder. A few big office blocks, a huddle of narrow streets teeming with humanity and a market where they sold anything and everything. At the east of the island jutted the slender tail of Catta Point, rocky and barren. Hua Range formed the spine and nestling side by side lay the twin lakes of Norri and Tai, their depths reflecting the changing sky. Middleton lay to the south of the range on a neat plateau looking as if cut out of the hillside for the express purpose of planning a town. There the new hospital had been built in perfect surroundings, but neither big enough nor modern enough to fill all its needs. There, also, Nigel had his private practice.

The slopes below it were tree dressed with cedars, magnolias, wild mangoes and jacarandas, while down in the valley were plantations of nutmeg and sugar cane. There were smaller plantations of bananas and little holdings where the country folk grew crops of fruit and vegetables to sell in the nearest markets.

North of Hua Range was the airfield and here the soil was poor, the land rocky, except at Marisha where, in the season, tourists filled the hotels. Here there were swimming pools, American bars complete with hot dogs and hamburgers and as many trappings as possible to tempt American dollars. Robert said it was obvious the English could not afford to go there or there would have been fish and chips.

The days slipped by rapidly. Nigel was

working at full speed and Robert persuaded them to stay on with him. It was foolish, he said, to think of getting a place of their own until Mary was absolutely fit. Besides, Boston Bay was a beauty spot on the south of the island, the swimming perfect and there wasn't a spot of land to be bought there. If they argued he'd get himself a flat in York City and they wouldn't like that, but it would be more sensible than for them to hunt for anything just now. The house was more suitable for a family than for a man alone.

Mary accepted the situation happily, knowing how much he enjoyed having them and the children were no trouble. They spent a great deal of their time on the beach with Della. She spent hours teaching Tony to swim and even little Judith could manage a few strokes. Martha, the housekeeper, had found them a seventeen-year-old girl to help and already Judith was happy with her although Tony clearly preferred to be with Della. Carmen was 'all right,' he said, but she couldn't swim very well. Mary had a delicate apricot tan and her cheeks were rosy and she had put on a little weight. Her brown hair was bleached by sun and salt water and happiness had given her a glow. Robert was more contented than he had been since Christine died.

One thing alone worried Mary. Try as she would she could not suppress that first feeling of aversion she had felt towards Della. There was no logical reason for it.

The girl was eagerly friendly and solicitous for her health. The continual, 'Are you feeling all right?' narked her almost beyond endurance. In an effort to overcome her dislike she went out of her way to be kind and let her be with the children as much as she wished. After all, Robert and Nigel looked on her as part of the family and it would be churlish to do anything else. In doing that she stored up more trouble than she would have thought possible. She accepted the fact that Nigel had little time and when Robert managed an occasional afternoon off to take both her and Ann for a drive she was delighted. More often than not the children would be left with Della and Carmen for they were too young to be interested in the layout of a town or the glory of Administrative offices—which cost far too much to run! But they took them to see a ship being loaded in Port Roy and to the hospital at Middleton where they were made a tremendous fuss of and given tea in Matron's room.

On one, only too rare, evening Nigel had taken Mary to the pictures and the children were in bed. Robert and Ann were sitting companionably on the veranda when Della came over. She was wearing a full-skirted pale pink dress and her hair hung loose round her shoulders. She had never put it up since the day they went to the airport.

'Where have you been in the evenings, young woman? You haven't been over for days. What have you been up to?'

'You've a suspicious mind, Uncle Robert. I've been out every evening.' There was an edge on her laugh. 'Paul's asked me to go to the dance at the Metro and we wondered if Mary and Nigel would like to come. Mary is looking much better and Nigel has hardly taken her anywhere.'

'They've gone to the pictures but I'll tell them you asked. You're right, my dear, it's time Mary met more people. We'll have to do something about it. How is Paul? I haven't seen him for a long time.'

'He's fine and like Nigel, thinks more of his work than anything!'

'Not so much that he doesn't want to take you dancing!' Robert chuckled.

'An unusual swain,' said Ann after Della had gone, 'who thinks of asking a married couple to join them.'

'I don't suppose it was his idea at all,' answered Robert easily, 'but Della is a gregarious creature and I think she has grown very fond of Mary and the children and she is right, it is time you both met more people. It's time we gave a party.'

It was Ann and Robert who did all the arranging. The only one who refused the invitation was Gordon Grant.

'That,' said Robert to Ann, 'is a relief. He would hardly be the life and soul of the party. Sometimes I think he is a natural hermit. How Tante Marie stands him I can't think. Probably stays for Della's sake. She was housekeeper before he married. I don't know how he would have managed when Myra left had it not been for her.'

'I thought Della's mother was dead.'

'No, she left them when Della was four or five. Rumour had it she went back to Martinique with another man, but if so nobody ever saw him with her. It was all hushed up, for Della's sake I expect.'

'Poor child!' Ann felt a momentary sense of shame for her dislike of the girl, completely unaware of Mary's feeling about her.

★   ★   ★

Mary was on top of the world and as excited as a child about the party. Nigel insisted on her having a new dress and helped her to choose it. It was quite simple, high in the front to hide the fact that she was still a little thinner than she should be, but cut low at the back to show the smooth, lightly tanned skin. She tried it on in front of him on the night before the party and he held her at arm's length, his eyes lit with admiration.

'You look stunning and I'm glad I insisted on white. I shall probably burst with pride.'

Her eyes filled with tears and one spilled over and trickled down her cheek. He put a finger to it gently then took out his handkerchief and mopped her face as if she were a child.

'What is this in aid of? Don't you dare spoil your frock.'

'Oh, dear, unzip me. It's not in aid of anything. I suddenly realised how happy I am and how well I feel and I'm grateful.' She gave a childish sniff and he helped her out of her frock and cradled her in his arms.

'Well, I'm not crying, you silly child, and I'm grateful, too. Grateful that you are so fit and that I've got you and the children. Grateful Dad looks so happy and that we talked Ann into coming with us. Sweetheart, how lucky can one be? I'm the happiest man in the world.' Suddenly he picked her up in his arms and carried her to the bed.

* * *

Della was ready for the party and Tante Marie looked at her with something close to wonder in her eyes. She knew she was having a new frock made but she had refused to let Tante Marie see it until she was dressed. Tante Marie breathed a sigh of relief. She had expected something daringly sophisticated that would show off her ripening beauty and put every other woman in the shade but she had been wrong. It was in her favourite pale, blush pink, very girlish and utterly plain. Her hair was shining and hung round her shoulders in deep waves and her only jewellery the charm bracelet Nigel had given her.

'Well, Tante Marie, do you approve for once?' She spun round and Tante Marie saw she was even wearing a pair of simple, pale pink pumps with no heels. She looked very young and untouched by life. It was only the quick glance out of the lustrous eyes that rang a warning note, but it was gone in a flash, leaving once more the young, untouched girl.

'Of the get-up, yes, as long as there is no wickedness in your heart.'

'I don't know what you are talking about. You might tell me to enjoy myself for a change. Not that I care what you think. I'm late already.' Then, as if she had forgotten her last remark, she walked over to the window and leant out. 'Tante Marie, what's happened to the wind? There isn't a breath of air. Oh, God, it's hot!'

'Are you feeling all right, child! You don't usually feel the heat and it's no hotter tonight than it has been this past week.'

'No, I suppose not but the breeze has dropped and I like to hear it in the trees.' She stood quite still as if listening. 'It's time the Devil Wind started. I'd better go. I can hear the music.'

38

'Don't you want to go, honey?' Tante Marie was looking at her with deep compassion. 'There isn't any need to pretend with me.'

'Pretend! There's nothing to pretend about.' She glared at Tante Marie's pitying eyes. 'Don't you ever feel sorry for me. I always get what I want in the long run.'

Tante Marie let out a deep sigh. 'Take what you want, said the Lord, and pay for it. Take care the payment isn't too great.'

'You're an old fool!' At the door Della turned back. 'You are, you know, but mainly because it wouldn't matter what I did I believe you'd still love me.' She laughed and the note was young and gay and suddenly disarming. 'I believe if I stuck a knife in you it wouldn't make any difference.'

'Oh, go along!' The dark face lit up. 'Don't you go sticking knives in anyone, you little she-cat. I'm never sure if you're as innocent as a baby or if you know more than I ever will of life.'

The party was a wonderful success and so was Mary. Her warmth and friendliness was a pool of light round her and both Michael and Paul Lacrosse were lost in admiration and if Paul's admiration was partly because he felt she had removed Nigel from any part in Della's life he was hardly aware of it himself.

It was Mary's evening and Nigel never noticed that Della scarcely came near them until it was time to go and then, with Paul by her side, she came and thanked them for a lovely party. Nigel beamed at both of them.

'We've loved having you. Take her home safely, Paul, although it's only next door. Tony would break his heart if anything happened to his playmate. If he was a bit older he would be cutting you out.'

Della lifted her eyes to Nigel and for a moment the shutters were raised. There was a look of self-assured possession, idolatrous in its intensity. Then the shutters were down again. Mary was conscious that her heart was beating with tremendous thumps, as if she had seen something in the dark eyes that was profane. Making a desperate effort she pulled herself together. She was behaving like a child, afraid of the expression in a young girl's eyes. It was a trick of the light.

'You're looking very beautiful tonight, Della, thank you for coming.' At least, she thought, I do mean that. She is staggeringly beautiful. She took the girl's hand. 'What a lovely bracelet.'

Della smiled at her, amusement and mockery in her eyes.

'It was one of Nigel's presents.' She bent and kissed Mary and to Mary's horror she felt herself recoil. In that moment she knew the girl hated her with a deep hatred that came from an untamed heart.

'You should take a rest in the morning.

40

You're looking tired.'

The concern in Della's voice gave her an insane desire to giggle helplessly. She had enjoyed the evening so much and yet now she felt herself flagging, as if Della willed it and her aversion grew like a canker.

'Della's right.' Nigel put his arm round her. 'You do look tired. A good lie-in for you tomorrow.'

Mary stood quite still, she wanted to say, 'For God's sake, stop it. I was all right until Della put the thought into our minds.' It took all her self-control to smile.

'I'm a nut case.' said Robert to Ann later. 'I should have kept it to a small party. It was too big and it went on too long. I'm afraid it was too much for Mary.'

'Don't worry, I'll make sure she takes it easy for a day or two. Funny she didn't look tired until Della said she did or perhaps I didn't notice. Maybe I was enjoying myself too much to think of anything else.'

* * *

Mary stretched out on the bed luxuriously, dismissing Della from her thoughts. She was tired but it had been worth it. She watched Nigel undressing and smiled.

'I like your friends but I shall never remember their names except the two Lacrosse boys and Clinton Harcourt. He says

I can borrow any of his books about the island that I like.'

'Well I never. Collecting an admirer under my very nose!'

'I cheated a bit because I remembered you told me how keen he is on island history and I led up to it. I feel sorry for Paul. He is going to break his heart over Della.'

'M-m! It's a pity he is so serious. She's only a kid.'

'Don't be ridiculous, Nigel. Della is a woman and a very lovely one and knows just what she is doing. You must be quite blind.' It was the first time he had heard her speak sharply.

He was fastening the buttons of his pyjamas and paused for a moment and scratched his chin thoughtfully.

'Perhaps you're right. You know I can't think of her as anything but the kid next door. She's been in and out of the house as if she belonged here ever since her mother left. I wonder where she went? She was staggeringly beautiful. Darker than Della. Della is like her and yet different and I'm blessed if I know how.' He got into bed and turned out the light, slipping an arm under Mary's head. Suddenly there was a rustle in the leaves just outside of the window.

'Listen,' Mary whispered the words. 'The breeze is springing up again. It's just dawned on me that that is why I felt tired. It's the hottest day since I've been here. Isn't it marvellous the way there is usually a breeze to keep it from being too hot. It's a wonderful climate.'

'As long as we don't get more than a breeze. Some of the old Negroes say there is a devil in the south wind. It can blow for days on end and after a bit it tries your temper. I suppose that's where the saying comes from.'

'Nothing can try my temper just now.' Mary giggled. 'Oh, Lord, how smug that sounds, but I'm so happy.'

'Then go on being happy, my sweet.'

He slept by her side like a child but Mary was wakeful and suddenly restless. Why, she asked herself, when I am so happy, do I get het up inside about Della? Even the mention of her name begins to nark me. I've got so much. Supposing she hates me, supposing she loves Nigel? Is it her fault? Nigel is right. She is only a girl and she has a pathetic background. Am I so selfish that I can't spare kindness and love for her? If I gave her love and friendship freely would she begin to accept the situation? I may be the one who is mostly at fault.

But instinctively she knew it was not that. There was something about the girl that chilled her. Her lovely eyes could look as innocent as a child's and then suddenly, like a curtain raised, she saw something else, something almost evil. Dear God, she

43

thought, I am letting my imagination romp. But it was a long time before she slept.

CHAPTER THREE

Mary hated lying in bed, but the morning after the party she was tired and knew why. When she was enjoying herself it was easy to keep going until she was exhausted. If she had had the sense to sit down and relax halfway through the evening she would have been all right.

Della came up to see her and said she would go down to the beach with the children, but it was too rough for swimming.

'The Devil Wind is springing up but I love it. It was a lovely party last night. Do you mind if I give the children a picnic? There's a little cove on the other side of the bay. It's sheltered from the wind and there is a pool where they can paddle.'

'I'm sure they'll love it but don't let the little imps tire you out.'

Mary was determined to be sensible and push away those fantastic thoughts that had caught hold of her in the night. This morning Della's eyes were as innocent as her own children's and she could have kicked herself for her wild imagination. The wind was springing up and she listened to the little howls of glee it made in the trees. Perhaps that was how it got its name. It sounded like little devils laughing. Nothing to do with making people bad tempered. She got up and went to the window and felt it ruffling her hair. Why on earth was she lying in bed? She wasn't tired any more, the wind had given her back her zest. She took a shower and dressed lazily. Ann had gone shopping and when she went downstairs old Martha looked at her with disapproval.

'Miss Ann said you were to rest all morning. You done get yourself tired out last night.'

'I'm fine now, Martha. Everyone spoils me. I'm going for a little walk. If Miss Ann comes back tell her I won't be long.'

It's quite ridiculous, she thought, as she walked down the garden path, and if I'm not careful I shall make an invalid of myself. Tante Marie was standing at the gate of the Grant house and Mary stopped to chat. She liked Tante Marie.

'Della said you were in bed. Weren't you feeling well or was the party too much for you yet awhile?'

'I don't think it was either.' Mary laughed. 'Everyone fusses just because I was ill. I would have stayed in bed all day if I had taken any notice. I feel as right as rain. Isn't this breeze wonderful? I had to come out in it.'

45

'This is no breeze, Mrs. Norton. It's the beginning of the Devil Wind. It's from the south, not the west. Sometimes it only lasts days, sometimes for weeks and when that happens it dries everything up and makes men crazy.'

'Women, too, I hope!' Mary's smile was full of fun. 'Just to keep up with the men.'

Tante Marie chuckled. 'It's one of the island's silly superstitions. What it does when it lasts too long is to get on your nerves and make you bad tempered.'

'That's just what Nigel said last night. So far I like it. It's bucked me up. Last night it was so hot.'

'Don't go walking too far. The wind is more tiring than you think. You are looking much stronger than when you first came and it would be a pity to overdo it now. Take your time. There's another day tomorrow.'

'Tante Marie, don't you start fussing me, too, but thank you for your kindness just the same.'

She walked along the road that bordered the beach but away from the houses. Tante Marie interested her. She was very dark, with large, gentle eyes, a broad but shapely nose and wide, well-curved mouth. Her English was perfect and her manner not that of a servant. Of course she was the housekeeper, but there was more than that. It was as if she had a right to be there. More the mistress

46

than the housekeeper.

At the end of the bay the road ended but a path wound upward through a cluster of trees and the wind gave little howling whistles. It was the first time she had walked far for always Ann, Robert or Nigel insisted on her going by car, but she loved walking. Once out of the cluster of trees she could see for miles. She had been climbing gently without realising it and now the path wandered by a small plantation. A tiny, white-washed house stood back from the road and outside, sitting in a rocking chair was an old coloured man, his hair as white as the wall.

'Good morning,' she called, 'isn't it a lovely day?'

He ignored her and she shrugged her shoulders. A middle-aged woman came out of the door, a big basket full of washing balanced on her hip.

'Don't you take no notice of Papa, ma-am, when the Devil Wind starts to blow he's as bad tempered as an old crow.' Her mouth widened in a particularly sweet smile.

'What a good job it doesn't make us all the same! Where does this path lead?'

'A bit further on there's a fork. Left it leads to the main road that goes to Catta Point. Right it's just a path down to the little bay. Where you from?'

'I'm Mrs. Norton, Dr. Nigel's wife.'

The friendly smile left the woman's face.

47

'Then you shouldn't walk too far. It's a long way to the beach.'

'I'm enjoying it, thank you.' Mary walked on. Why, when she knew she was Nigel's wife did she lose that pleasant smile? Was there a special reason or was it because she had heard she had been ill and thought her a fool to be walking?

The smell of spices filled the air. Devil Wind indeed! This was just a warm breeze caressing her cheeks and bare arms. She forgot the time and that she would have the walk back. Forgot that Ann would come in from shopping and worry. This was the first time she had been alone for months and she was enjoying the sense of freedom it gave her. Down on the beach she sat on a rock and wished she had brought her bathing suit with her. Here the land curled round forming a natural breakwater and the sea was almost calm inside it. Behind her the high hill was rugged and almost bare. The sun poured down and there was no shelter. In a few minutes she realised she had been stupid to come so far. It was a long walk back to the shade of the trees and she would look a wreck and Ann would be concerned.

By the time she reached the top of the hill she was exhausted. The old man still sat outside the house but there was no sign of the woman. The old man rocked back and forth, seemingly indifferent to the heat. She longed for a drink of water but his malevolent glare stopped her. When she reached the trees she sat down and rested her back against one of them and drifted into sleep. It was an ugly sleep. She was overtired and although her body rested her mind took on a separate existence. The old man was chasing her with a stick in his gnarled hand and the woman stood by watching, making no move to help her. She woke up gasping with fright, realised there was no one near and began to laugh. That, she said, serves you right, Mary Norton, for not listening to words of warning! You should have done what you were told and spent the morning resting. She sat for a little while, gathering her strength and wished she had brought her watch. Please the Lord, Ann had taken longer over her shopping than she intended! When she got to her feet she was surprised to find how the rest had refreshed her in spite of the silly dream. She brushed down her dress and ran her fingers through her hair hoping she didn't look a mess.

Ann was fuming. 'Really, Mary, you must be daft to go walking when you were tired. Martha says you have been gone more than two hours. I've only just got back or I would have been looking for you.'

'Idiot!' Mary laughed. 'Why do you get into such a state? As a matter of fact I walked up to that cluster of trees and sat down and went to sleep. I'm sure it did me more good than lying in bed.' She never said how much farther she had gone. There wasn't any need for she was feeling fine. Even the silly dream had receded and seemed a figment of her imagination.

'As long as you've not tired yourself out.'

'If everyone keeps fussing you'll turn me into a hypochondriac or a semi-invalid.'

'Perhaps you're right,' Ann said grudgingly. 'You do look better. The trouble with me is that I'm a born fusser.'

'Well, don't go telling Nigel you were worried. He's bad enough without you to egg him on and what you two can't fuss about Dad can. I'm getting heartily sick of it. I've always been as strong as a horse. Old Dr. Fielding said I have the constitution of an ox or I wouldn't have got better. If there is any more mention of taking care I'll have hysterics and that would give you all a shock.'

Ann began to laugh, her pleasant face lit with amusement.

'That will be the day! Whatever we accuse you of we couldn't say you suffer from nervous heeby-jeebies.'

At half-past-four Della brought the children home. Little Judith climbed on to Mary's lap, tired and contented but Tony was in a bad temper. Della was apologetic.

'He's cross because he couldn't swim, but it was much too rough.'

50

Mary was on the point of asking why she hadn't thought of taking them to the little bay beyond the white cottage where the sea was calm but realised in time that no one knew she had been there.

'There'll be lots of other days when you can swim, Tony, there's no need to be cross.'

The small face with the rounded, childish contours stared back at her sullenly, then he turned on his heels and went out in the garden.

'Tony,' Mary called, 'come back at once.' His rudeness angered her beyond common sense. Usually he was an imp of mischief but reasonably tractable and seldom rude.

'I'm afraid it's my fault. I should have brought them home sooner but they were enjoying themselves so much it seemed a shame to spoil their fun. He's probably tired.' Della sounded innocently repentant but Mary was certain she was enjoying Tony's naughtiness and her anger rose higher.

I've been too wrapped up in myself for months, she thought. First the illness and then Nigel. I mustn't lose my temper. Whatever Ann says I must spend more time with the children. They'll forget I'm their mother and authority rests with me.

'I expect I've been spoiling them a bit but I do love being with them. They're such fun but I'll try to be more sensible in future.' Della gave a rueful smile. 'I must run. I've

51

got a lot of things to do and I'm going out with Paul this evening.'

'Then have a good time.' Mary seethed, certain the girl was inwardly laughing at her but there was nothing she could say. On the surface she was giving her time generously but she was sure there was a reason behind it, but what?

'I always do. If the wind drops I'll take the children swimming tomorrow. Tony is already like a fish in the water.' She did not ask if she could, it was as if she had a right.

'I wonder what she has to do?' Ann was watching Della run along the path to the Grant house. 'I thought all she did was to have a good time.'

'Don't you like her, Ann?'

'She gets under my skin. Probably I'm just plain jealous of her youth and beauty. A figure and face that could stop the traffic in Trafalgar Square.' She gave a sudden amused grin. 'Maddening when you never manage to get a second glance yourself. I suppose when you are as lovely as that you can't help getting a bit arrogant. I don't know.'

But that wasn't the reason she disliked Della although she couldn't tell Mary. She didn't trust her and was sure she was in love with Nigel. If she could have warned Mary without saying too much she might have done, but Robert loved the girl almost like a daughter and Nigel was fond of her.

Mary was still sitting with Judith on her knee, the fair head nestling against her shoulder. Forget all about Della and concentrate on the children. It would work itself out before long and no doubt Della would soon tire of playing nursemaid.

At bedtime she took Judith up for her bath. Ann didn't argue for she could see Mary was eager to get back to a normal life and she was right. They had been curbing her too much and she was an energetic woman and it must be irksome. There was splashing and laughing from the bathroom and she smiled. In a week or two's time she must begin to think of going back to England or getting a job. She didn't really want to leave the island yet. Perhaps Robert could give her some ideas.

Mary came downstairs flushed and smiling. 'Thank goodness I'm allowed to be a mother again. This climate suits Judith. She's looking wonderful. Where's my naughty little son?'

'Riding the bicycle round the garden path.'

The two women went on to the veranda and Mary called him. He ignored her completely. The anger which she had suppressed began to rise again and she went down to the path and waited. As he pedalled towards her she stepped in his way and he made to ride round her. She grabbed his arm and he was forced to stop. The bicycle fell on the path.

'Tony, when I call you you are to come at once.'

'I don't want to.'

'I don't care what you want, you are to come. It's time for your bath and bed.'

He struggled to get away but although Mary was small she was strong. Suddenly he began to fight like a young tiger.

'Let me alone! I want to play.' His voice rose in a scream. 'Let go, let go!'

Mary was incensed and, bending over, smacked his leg sharply.

'You little horror, you'll do as you are told and at once.'

Sobbing and pulling away from her he was finally dragged into the house and up the stairs. Ann watched anxiously. She didn't want Mary to tire herself but she knew this was a battle of wills between mother and son and it was best not to interfere. By the time Tony was in the bath, still sobbing and screaming, Mary felt as if she hadn't a scrap of energy left. He refused to let her wash him and she sat down on the stool exhausted. Never before had she had such a scene with him and she was furious not only with her son but with herself for having allowed him to get so out of hand. Tears of anger poured down her cheeks. It was at this moment that Nigel came into the bathroom.

'Good heavens, I thought all the devils in the wind were centred in here! What is all the

54

row about? Tony, what have you been up to?'

Mary was boiling with rage. 'This is my business. He's my son and he's got to learn to do as I tell him.'

'Of course he has,' Nigel was being reasonable which didn't help, 'but he's mine, too, and I won't have you upset.'

'It's nothing to do with you.' Mary knew she was saying the wrong thing but with her temper uppermost she didn't care. 'I'm quite capable of handling him.'

'You happen to be my wife and I won't have you making yourself ill over a naughty little boy.'

Mary was about to tell him to get out of the bathroom when she caught the expression on the child's face. There was complete triumph, knowing he was the centre of a storm.

'Then you'd better cope,' she answered. Leaving them together she went to the bedroom. Flinging herself on the bed she burst into a torrent of tears. She and Nigel had never had words before and although Tony was no angel he had never behaved so badly. Her sobs gradually subsided. All was quiet apart from the sound of Nigel's voice drifting in through the open door. A quarter of an hour later he came into the room and sat on the side of the bed. Gently stroking her hair he waited until he was sure she was listening.

'Now what is all this about? I've never seen

you upset like this and if you do it often you'll wear yourself out.'

'Didn't you know I'm a bad tempered shrew and if you say one more word about wearing myself out I'll scream. Everyone is so beastly cocksure about what I should do. Nobody, but nobody, seems to think I am capable of bringing up my own children and what happens? Tony is spoilt rotten.' She was almost enjoying herself. 'He's become a little horror and wants a damn good hiding.'

'I should think he had that. There are the marks of your fingers on his leg.' Nigel was trying to be reasonable but he was shocked. He never thought Mary could be spiteful. Anyone would think the child was a delinquent—just because he had a bit of a tantrum!

Mary lay quite still. Nigel's words had drawn out all her temper and she had had no idea she had hit the child so hard. After a while she turned on her back and looked at Nigel out of tear-red eyes.

'I'm sorry. I didn't mean to get so angry. It seemed as if Tony wasn't mine any more and his naughtiness was just the spur I needed to go haywire. I don't remember losing my temper like that for years and years. He was very naughty.'

'What happened?'

She explained simply but her voice was still blurred after her passion of weeping. Nigel's heart warmed. She looked like an anxious child, eager for understanding.

'You know he has been spoilt. All those weeks I was in hospital it must have been difficult for Ann not to give into them more than I used to and then Della admitted she has been doing the same. He was in a temper because it was too rough for him to swim.'

'Not to worry, darling. You are right, we've been fussing you too much. It is time you had the children more to yourself.' He bent and kissed her. 'I've the whole day tomorrow and I'll take you and the young monkeys over to Marisha Bay for a picnic. Let me tell you something. The Devil Wind looks like dropping so Tony should be his own sweet self once more.' He grinned at her and she gave a sudden chuckle.

'You and your Devil Wind. Perhaps that is what was wrong with me! Nigel, did I mark Tony's leg badly?'

'No, it will be gone by morning and kids are seldom resentful of a hard slap when they know they deserve it. But, darling, go easy on him. Remember it is quite a while since you held a firm maternal hand and he may get awkward if it comes down too suddenly.'

'Do you think I should go and kiss him good night?'

'He was almost asleep when I left him so I should stay where you are and rest a little longer. That party was too much.'

'Shut up! It wasn't the party and I never felt tired until Della told me I looked it.'

He burst out laughing. 'Do you think she put some hypnotic influence on you?'

'What made you say such a thing?' There was an edge to her voice at the thought. Then she saw the funny side and joined in the laughter. 'You and your nonsense! I've just realised what did make me tired. I'd had three gin slings and in spite of being a journalist I'm not used to them. I've a feeling I was almost tight.'

'Don't tell me I've married a toper as well as a shrew!'

He cradled her in his arms and the world steadied. For a few awful moments she had wished she hadn't married him in such a hurry. Now all was right again.

★   ★   ★

Ann watched them go off on their picnic and breathed a sigh of relief that Mary was looking almost like her old self. She had had a chat with Robert the night before and he had encouraged her to look for work.

'Don't go back to England, Ann, we need you here.'

'Not to help in the house. Old Martha's let me do some of the shopping but that's about all. She rules her helpers with a rod of iron and everything runs on oiled wheels.'

Robert smiled. 'Christine had a marvellous power of organisation and she trained her well. Candidly there is a great need here for welfare workers and you should have little difficulty in finding a post although it may not be immediately. You'd be doing work you are used to and be on hand if Mary needs you.'

'I don't think she does any more. We've been doing our best to make an invalid of her and she's beginning to get irritated.'

'Come to town with me tomorrow and I'll introduce you to one or two people who may be able to help. I'm sorry you're not a secretary. Mine is leaving to get married!'

'No shorthand or typewriting much as I should enjoy working for you. I'll meet you for lunch and then I can potter round in York for a while.'

★ ★ ★

Tony had completely recovered from his bad temper and was delighted to be with Nigel, but he watched Mary with wary eyes. It was almost as if he didn't trust her but during the day it wore off and he was cock-a-hoop to show off his swimming.

'He's had good tuition,' Nigel said. 'Della's about the best swimmer on the island. She swam almost before she could walk.'

Della, Della, Mary thought. Her name crops up continually! She pushed the thought

59

away, knowing that if she was not careful the girl would become an obsession with her. In the afternoon she lay on a rug and slept solidly for an hour, waking with a twinkle in her eyes and an exuberant feeling of good health. Nigel was sitting by her side, his back against a rock. The children were digging a sandpit.

'Why did I ever fuss you? You've got an aptitude for relaxing if you are left alone. You were snoring like a grampus!'

'I don't know what a grampus is and I don't snore!'

'You don't know what you do when you are asleep, Funny Face, but I've never seen you look so fit. I begin to feel as if I am the one who needs looking after! Gosh, I needed this day off. Things have been hectic for the past week. We could do with two more doctors at the hospital and another in the practice. Thank goodness young March has nearly finished his year as houseman at St. Joseph's. He'll be back in a couple of months.'

'Is that Nurse March's brother?'

'Yes, and he's a brilliant boy and his sister a dedicated nurse. Pity she couldn't have been a doctor.'

'I didn't realise things are so difficult. Why didn't you tell me?'

'I suppose I've learnt to take it for granted. There's a shortage of most things. Good opportunities mostly. Not enough money and a great deal of what there is in the wrong hands. Dad would have come to England with me for a couple of months had he not put his spare cash into helping young March through medical school.'

'And I hadn't any idea.'

'Why should you, sweet? Dad didn't want it shouted from the housetops. Jimmy March's father has worked for Dad for years and he's a fine man. Dad isn't badly off but he doesn't make a fortune. Being a solicitor on Huahnara is not the most paying game and he doesn't traffic in side lines.'

'It's time I learned a little more about the island. I've been lazing around with my head in the sand.'

He ran his fingers through her hair. 'And you've got most of it in your untidy mop. Do you know there was one disadvantage in getting married so quickly. We couldn't have a honeymoon. It's time we went home. Let's get the children to bed and if you don't feel too tired we'll go to the Metro to dinner.'

'After that sleep! Not so likely.'

Mary bathed Judith and tucked her up and left Tony to Nigel. Not even to him could she admit that she was afraid of another storm although Tony appeared to have recovered his own good humour. Once in bed she kissed him good night but there wasn't the old warmth in his kiss and he didn't fling his arms round her as he used. She wondered if

61

she was exaggerating his coolness. It wasn't really to be wondered at. She had had so little to do with the children for months and he naturally resented her putting her foot down. Nigel was right, she must go carefully. Judith was different. She was younger and an easy child at any time.

She and Nigel sat at a table tucked away in the corner of the roof garden at the Metro. The many coloured fairy lights gave a sense of carnival and Mary realised how much she and Nigel needed a little time to themselves. Perhaps Nigel needed it even more than she did. It wasn't easy for a man to marry a woman who already had a couple of children.

'When things are easier at the hospital it would be nice if we could have a few days honeymoon.'

Nigel's words were almost an extension of her own thoughts. The light was too dim for her to see the expression in his eyes but she knew what they would look like. They were such a startling blue and although he was only thirty there were already tiny lines etched round them.

'I know it's not usual to take children on a honeymoon but they'd love it.' There was laughter in his voice.

'That's about the nicest thing you could say, but we'll make some other arrangements for the little horrors. I have no intention of taking them on a honeymoon! Apart from loving you very much you are about the nicest man I know. You always speak of them as ours and I love it.'

'In spite of the fact that last night you informed me in no uncertain terms that Tony was your son?'

'It was a beastly thing to say.'

'No, you were upset and it was natural although I must admit that for a little while I was flaming mad. Let's forget it. Tonight you are a dream of delight and I could eat you so you had better watch out. Let's dance or I shall behave like a raging wolf. Just imagine what excitement it would cause if the respectable Dr. Norton seized his wife in his arms and began to smother her with passionate kisses!'

By the time they were dancing Mary had recovered from her laughter. It was a night to remember. She had never been so happy before, even when she and Barry were first married. Nigel's youth and gaiety were uppermost and her own years dropped away. She had no idea she was looking almost beautiful and very young. Happiness was welling in her like a flood. Nigel's arms were close and protective and she knew he was giving her something she had never known before. Barry had loved her dearly but it was a quiet love, without the fire she knew now. How lucky can I be, she thought? Half an hour later Nigel said it was time they went home.

'But I'm not tired!'

'Who said you were? I just remarked it was time we went home and that was not because I considered you tired! Lord, woman, the only excuse I have for putting my arms round you here is to dance!'

'Sir, are you making improper suggestions?' She giggled.

'Really! What are women coming to! You shock me!'

As they were leaving Della and Paul came on to the roof.

'Don't say you are going?' Della looked at them with lustrous eyes. She was wearing a flame-coloured dress which accentuated the honey-brown of her skin. 'It's early yet. Paul and I have only just come.'

'What it is to be young!' Nigel was bubbling. 'You forget, child, Mary and I are an old married couple and I have to be up in the morning early. Enjoy yourselves.'

'Good gracious, and the night before you left for England you danced with me until two in the morning!'

The look Della gave him was passionately loving and more. For a brief space it was determinedly possessive. Paul's boyish smile faded. Mary looked at the girl's flaming beauty and her heart beat swiftly, like a bird's wing fluttering in her breast. Fear and jealousy were mixed. Nigel alone was untouched, his heart too full of happiness.

'That was before I had responsibilities and before you were old enough to go out alone with anyone younger than big brother.' He grinned cheerfully.

'Poor old thing!' Della's rich laugh rang out. 'But it would be silly to let Mary get tired.' She was suddenly sympathetic and Mary felt a spurt of anger. Damn the girl! Why must she forever harp on that as if she had one foot in the grave?

In the car she settled at Nigel's side. Absurd to let the girl annoy her so but her possessive air and her allusion to an evening spent with Nigel was deliberate and she hadn't cared how much Paul was hurt. Instinctively she knew the girl cared for no one but herself and wished desperately she were not so much part and parcel of the Norton household.

CHAPTER FOUR

The wind from the south dropped as suddenly as it had started and there was a gentle breeze from the west. Mary was feeling as fit as a fiddle. Ann had not yet got a post but she had met a number of people and Robert was sure that before too long she would get something suitable.

For two weeks they saw practically nothing of Della and it was Ann or Mary or both of them who went to the beach with Carmen and the children. Tony was his old mischievous self again and Mary began to think Nigel had been right—she had put her foot down too quickly, but he was now beginning to realise that she was again holding the reins. Carmen was extremely good with both the children, patient and gentle but quite firm and she was fast becoming an asset.

The weather was absolutely perfect and Mary had another reason for happiness. She was almost certain she was pregnant. She longed for at least two more children and the sooner the better. She wondered why Della had not been near and was relieved but at the same time anxious. She knew how fond Robert and Nigel were of her and had an uncomfortable feeling that they might blame her because she was no longer running in and out. Stop worrying, she told herself, you're damn well hunting for trouble. If she comes you don't like it and if she doesn't you imagine all kinds of unpleasant consequences. Ann didn't mention her and privately thought the more she stayed away the better. Ann had an aptitude for being honest with herself.

'What about taking the children for a picnic to Marisha, Mary? It would be a change and we might as well make the most of the chance before Tony starts school.'

Robert had given Nigel a lift to the hospital so that there was a car free for Ann and Mary.

'Would you be an angel and take them on your own? There are one or two things I want to do.' Mary wanted to be on her own to savour the joy of her hoped for pregnancy. 'Now don't fuss, Ann, I'm feeling fine and I want to sort out some clothes. I must think about getting some for Tony, too. He's growing at a terrific rate. Oh, dear, I'm being a selfish blighter, putting the young monkeys on you and it's Carmen's day off.'

'Don't be silly. I'd love to take them if you are sure you don't mind.'

'Of course I don't. I'm going to enjoy being a bad mother and push them off on you and young Tony is behaving much better these days. Perhaps because there is no Devil Wind blowing.' They both laughed for the Devil Wind had become a joke between them.

After they had gone she sat on the veranda and did some mending then she went up to her room and tidied a couple of drawers. By that time she realised she had hours ahead of her and had nothing to do but dream and what she needed was some exercise. She was absolutely fit now and it would be pleasant to explore the little bay past the white house. This time she had the sense to take a shady hat with her remembering how little protection there was.

The old man was again sitting outside as if

he had never moved since she saw him last but there was no sign of the woman. It was strange how uninhabited this spot seemed. No other houses, not a soul on the path. She wondered if it was all private property but there was no notice anywhere.

Once she was certain of her pregnancy she would do some househunting. Near the hospital for preference so that Nigel could come in for meals. Sometimes she wondered if he stopped to eat at all during the day for there was not only the hospital but the private patients. Since the evening they had danced at the Metro he had been working all hours. If he came home for dinner he was usually late and often he would go out again and not get home until midnight. She had known that a doctor's life was not his own, but in the last two weeks they had hardly had any time together, certainly no time to talk for as soon as his head touched the pillow he was asleep.

The sand was dazzling white in the sunshine and the water a brilliant blue except at the edges where it rippled and foamed like lace. She sat on the sand and rested her back against a rock, tipping her hat over her eyes to protect them from the glare. It was utterly peaceful. Tomorrow she would bring Ann and the children but today she was glad to be alone. It gave her time to think, to be herself. The walk hadn't seemed half as far today, probably because she was now quite fit. The children would adore it and they could collect shells for here there were so many and so varied.

After a while she wished she had had the sense to tell Martha where she was going and bring sandwiches and a drink. The heat was greater than she had expected and she was thirsty. Another few minutes and she must make a move.

It wasn't until she began to climb the hill from the beach that she realised how hot it was. The sun was at its height, sweat was beginning to trickle down her back and between her breasts. Her arms were hot and dry and there was no shade at all until she could reach the trees. It was idiotic to think it would be a good place to picnic. The walk and the intense heat would wear the children out. Her heart was beating rapidly and the sun on her back was making her feel desperately sick—or perhaps it was her pregnancy. She was out of her mind to have come for it was much hotter than it had been on her previous visit. If only she could reach the little house. She didn't care tuppence how unfriendly the old man and the woman were. She must rest. Struggling on for a few more yards she lurched to the side of the road and was violently sick. Utterly drained of energy she stumbled on until she reached the fence of the house. She leant on it, too exhausted to walk up the path and ask if she might have a glass of water and rest. The house rocked backwards and forwards in a silly sort of rhythm and she closed her eyes. Just as she was slipping to the ground she felt an arm round her and blinked in an effort to focus clearly. Della's great, dark eyes were looking into hers.

'It's all right, Mary, I'm here. Hold on a moment and I'll get the gate open.'

Vaguely she felt a strong arm guiding her along the path. She didn't see the old man still sitting in his rocking chair. When she opened her eyes she was lying on a bed in a darkened room. It was astonishingly cool and heaven to relax. Della was sitting by her side.

'Are you feeling better now?'

'Yes, thank you. I must have been mad to walk so far in the heat. I'm not used to it.'

'Don't talk any more. I'll get you a drink.'

It was a cool, dark liquid in a thick glass and it was like nectar. She drank it gratefully and in a few minutes she drifted into a light sleep, so light that she could hear voices although she couldn't understand what they were saying. It wasn't until she wakened properly that she realised they were talking in the local patois which she could hear through the open door. Nigel had told her it was still used by some of the older people but she was surprised to hear Della using it. Suddenly she broke into English.

'You and Tante Marie are old fools, Cassy.'

70

The rich, velvety voice was biting.

'We may be fools, Miss Della, but that's all we are.'

'I know. You should have let Papa Dan teach you instead of Father O'Donnell.'

'You take that Mrs. Norton home. She's a nice woman.'

'You should have been a nun. I'll go and wake her.'

Mary closed her eyes and when Della touched her she opened them slowly. Clearly she had not been meant to hear the conversation. Not that it mattered. She couldn't make head nor tail of it.

'Do you feel better now, Mary?'

'Yes, I'm fine. I don't even feel tired. What an idiot I was. Have I been asleep long?'

'Only about half an hour.'

'I must get home. Martha will be worried.'

'I'll come with you.'

Mary thanked the woman and she gave a brief, 'You're welcome!' Then she thanked the old man who was now sitting in the cool living-room. He grinned at her, showing toothless gums, but said nothing. She wondered if he could speak English.

She and Della walked to the cluster of trees and it wasn't until they reached them that Della spoke.

'Mary, please don't say anything to anyone about this or there'll be a row at home. You see Cassy is Tante Marie's half sister and

71

Papa Dan their father. Tante Marie is proud of being a housekeeper and doesn't like anyone to know she comes from a poor family. She hates me going there but I've known Papa Dan since I was a little kid and I'm fond of him. He may not look very bright but he's a clever old man. Tante Marie would be furious if she thought you had been there.'

'Of course I won't say anything. Besides, I don't want anyone to know I was such a fool. I'd be in for more trouble than you and they'd fuss for days, bless them. I'll be careful not to walk too far in future.'

'Yes, you'll need to be. This climate doesn't suit everyone. You looked dreadful when you got to Papa Dan's but you look better now.' She paused for a moment. 'Would you like me to come in with you? It would stop Martha pestering you with questions.'

'I feel rather like a naughty child but it would be nice not to have Martha looking as if I need a scolding.' Little as she liked Della she was grateful. She must try and be more friendly. 'Where have you been lately? We've seen nothing of you.'

'Didn't Nigel tell you?' There was amusement and definite triumph in the rich voice. 'I'm doing voluntary work at the hospital. They're very short-staffed and although I don't know much about it there is a lot I can do. I'm getting quite good at taking

round bedpans and pushing trolleys. Are you
sure you feel well enough to walk all the way
without a rest?'

'Quite sure.'

'I'm surprised Nigel hasn't told you for I
know he is pleased I'm helping even if it is
only odd jobs, just filling in where I'm
needed. You've no idea how hard he works.'

'I've a good idea. I was his patient you
know.'

'Of course and he gets anxious about you.
It was a good job I had this morning off or I
wouldn't have been at hand, would I? I'm on
duty again this evening to help the night
staff.'

Mary looked at her thoughtfully, convinced
she had taken on this work to be near Nigel.
She felt rising anger against him for not
having told her himself. Had he suggested she
should work there?

Martha was irate. Lunch was spoiled and
she had been worried. Her brown face was
shrewish. It was Della who soothed her, lying
with such aplomb that Mary was staggered.
Mary had met her on the beach, they had
shared sandwiches and forgot the time.

'It was better than having her nag you and
these old servants do get a bit above
themselves. If I were you I would have a rest
and be fresh for this evening.'

'You're probably right. If you are going to
work this evening you should do the same.'

73

'I don't need to.' Della was already at the door. 'I'm never tired.'

Mary knew she was flaunting her youth and health and longed to make a cutting reply but knew it would be stupid even if she could think of one and she couldn't. She wondered what Nigel would think if he knew the ease with which the girl could lie. All feeling of gratitude had gone. The girl had enjoyed making her feel sick and inadequate.

When she had washed the dust and sand off she stretched out on her bed and took herself to task. She was getting super-sensitive over this business of health and more than super-sensitive over Della. She allowed everything the girl said to annoy her. Suppose Nigel had suggested she should do some work at the hospital? What did it matter? It was ridiculous to get worked up if anyone mentioned her health. Dr Maddison, the senior physician, had given her a clean bill of health.

'You tiny women are deceptive.' He had smiled. 'You manage to look delicate and frail but you stand up to a terrific amount. Often far better than the robust looking ones. Forget all about your illness and I'll tell Nigel to stop fussing. Your heart and lungs are absolutely sound. There's no earthly reason why anyone should treat you like an invalid.'

The episode this morning had been her own fault and was probably a touch of the sun

74

made worse by her pregnancy. She hugged the thought to her heart. Nigel would be thrilled. She was hungry and wished Della had not told Martha she had eaten. Oh, well, she would make up for it later. She dropped off to sleep but dream after unpleasant dream haunted her and they were all connected with the little white house and the old man. He didn't do anything, just stared at her but there was something in the old face that was terrifying. The toothless mouth grinned evilly and the sunken eyes stared into hers. She wakened feeling sick and frightened. It was nearly time for Ann and the children to come home and she must look fresh and bright for them. She put on a clean white dress and carefully touched up her pale cheeks with a little rouge. Whatever happened Ann mustn't know about this morning or that she was feeling a bit under the weather.

Over at the Grant house Della was also lying on her bed, her hands behind her head and her eyes closed. At half-past-four Tante Marie came into the room. Della opened her eyes.

'What do you want?'

'To know what you are up to. You've hardly been inside the house for the last two weeks and this morning I saw you go towards Papa Dan's and you came back with Mrs. Norton. If you are up to mischief I'll find out from Cassy.'

'What should I be doing? I just went to see Papa Dan. That is more than you bother to do.'

'Don't start pretending to me. Papa Dan is a wicked old man and well you know it. What was Mrs. Norton doing to be coming from that way? Don't tell me you are encouraging her to see him.'

'Don't be such a fool. She's a silly woman and had walked down to the little beach and it was too much for her. I saw her leaning on the fence and then she fainted. I just took her inside until she was better. She asked me not to tell anyone in case they started fussing her but you have to find out everything. I don't think she'll take such a walk again. Nigel must have been daft to marry her. She hasn't any stamina.'

'Rubbish. She's just tiny. I know. How many lies are you telling? You want her to be sick, you wicked child.' Tante Marie was standing by the bed, glowering down at her. 'When will you put Nigel out of your head? He loves his wife and he's happy with her.'

'Is he?' Della smiled. 'He'll never be really happy with her. He'll soon get tired. She's old and colourless.'

'Della, don't try me too far. Was Cassy out when you were there?'

'Yes,' Della laughed, 'but don't go getting crazy ideas. She was back before we left. Those two are funny. There's old Papa Dan weaving his spells and Cassy praying to the Virgin for his soul.'

'Cassy's a good woman.'

'I know and so does Papa Dan and she's deadly boring. Who do you pray for, Tante Marie? My soul or your own? Don't bother about mine. If I have one it can take care of itself. I'm going out this evening and I won't be back until late.'

'Where are you going?'

'That's my business.'

'Perhaps it is a good thing for Paul Lacrosse that you don't want to marry him. He's a good boy and you'd make a bad wife.'

Della narrowed her eyes. 'Don't be too sure I won't. If I married him I could do as I liked without you around to interfere.'

'Della, Della, can't you think of someone but yourself for once.'

Tante Marie knew that she had no intention of marrying Paul. It was only said to bait her and her heart ached with love and yet quaked with terror. Why couldn't she be like other girls of her age. Fun loving, perhaps a bit selfish but with no evil in her heart.

'Be careful, Tante Marie, or I may start thinking of you and you might not like that. Would you like me to put the evil eye on you?' Della's eyes were full of mockery.

Tante Marie went down to the kitchen and berated young Nina for nothing in particular. Nina shrugged her slim shoulders. Something

77

had upset her but it wouldn't last for Tante Marie was kind at heart. On a whole she liked working at the Grant house. It was a good place and work wasn't easy to get out of season. It was easier when the tourists came but it only lasted four or five months at the most and this was all the year round. Besides, there were four little ones at home and her father was out of work again. Tante Marie made sure everything was going along nicely in the kitchen and then went to her own room. She knelt in front of the tiny statue of the Virgin and prayed earnestly. Perhaps the Sweet Lady would forgive her her sins. Dear Cassy, she knew how hard her half sister prayed for both her and Papa Dan and surely the Virgin would listen to her. If she envied anyone at all it was Cassy because she was at peace with the Church.

Later she watched Della get into her car and drive off. It went at a terrific speed and a dreadful thought came unbidden. Perhaps Della would kill herself and her mischief would be at an end. Then she fell on her knees again and prayed the Sweet Lady would take such evil from her heart.

Gordon Grant was sitting in the cool lounge poring over some newly acquired stamps when she slipped up to the little house. Cassy was sewing. Tante Marie never spoke patois. She had forgotten most of it years before. The old man was in bed and Cassy was working by

78

the light of an oil lamp.

'Cassy, you shouldn't be working by this light. It's bad for your eyes.'

'We have to eat.'

'If only you would let me help. You know I've got the money.'

Cassy shook her head. 'No, Marie, I can manage. Why have you come? To ask what Della wanted this morning? I don't know any more than you do.'

'Had she been here long when you came in?'

'I don't know. Mrs. Norton had only just come because as I came in the door I heard Della tell her to rest for a while and she would feel better. She told me that she had seen her holding on to the fence and when she got down to her she fainted so there was nothing she could do but bring her in.'

'Where did she take her to rest?'

'Where do you think? Into Papa's room. Those two are up to some wickedness. Mrs. Norton came past here once before. She looked tired but I wouldn't ask her in because I knew who she was. Marie, the Good Lord doesn't want us to think bad of anyone but Della is wicked. Can't you keep her away from Papa, she makes him worse!' The dark eyes filled with tears. 'I pray so hard for him and Father O'Donnell says his naughty ways are only silly superstition but I don't know. If I annoy him he says my head will ache and my eyes hurt and before long they do.'

'Don't be silly, Cassy. Father O'Donnell is right. It's only silly superstition. Papa frightens you into having a headache and your eyes hurt because you will sew at night. If you'd let me help you you wouldn't have to work so late.'

Cassy shook her head. She had her own standards and Marie didn't insist or perhaps her sins would fall on her sister's head!

As she walked home she clasped her hands and prayed. Was Della just a naughty, spoilt child? If only she would fall in love with another man and stop being foolish over Nigel, if only Paul were not so bewitched by her because then he might have more control and stop being a doormat. She needed a strong man who would love her and keep her in order, but Marie knew there had been other men in her life and she had always been stronger than they.

Della's room was tidy. She always put her things away neatly and stormed if anyone touched them. Tante Marie opened one drawer after another and every one was in perfect order. Her heart ached. Poor child, she had loved Nigel since she was a child until it was an obsession, but when she realised it was no use she would give up. She remembered the misery on her face when she knew he was married. If only he had had the sense to break it gently, but men were such fools and she was sure he had no knowledge of her love for him. Marie was fond of Nigel and what she had seen of his wife she liked, but she loved Della like she would have done her own child. The child didn't mean any real harm but her passionate heart was hurt and when people were hurt they hit out. Didn't she remember her own agony?

It was the handkerchief drawer that made her pause. There was a little lump under the neatly arranged squares of linen and lace. The tiny wax doll lay under them, a pin pushed into a spot in the centre just below the ribs. It was beautifully made and she even imagined a likeness to Mary Norton. She stared at it in horror, afraid to touch it. All the old superstitions crowded into her mind. This was voodoo and should have died in the island long ago. For a time she stared at it, not knowing what to do, her fears multiplying. It was minutes before she could bring herself to lift the tiny image. When she did she took it gently in her hands and eased out the pin in sheer, black terror as if she might injure the woman it was supposed to represent. Then she carried it to her room and locked the door. Putting the doll on the altar in front of the light that always burned in front of the Virgin she fell on her knees and prayed for a long time. Afterwards she hid the doll in a drawer and locked it, putting the key on a long ribbon round her neck and hiding it between her breasts.

CHAPTER FIVE

Mary was sitting on the veranda when Ann brought the children home. They were tired but happily content. Mary was feeling sick and blaming herself for missing her lunch. She wished Della hadn't been so skilful with her lies for she would have asked Martha to get her something light to eat. Convinced the sickness was caused by hunger she tucked into tea with the children. Ann was amused and looked at her with approval.

'You've got your old appetite back, thank goodness. I wouldn't dare eat sandwiches like that or I'd get as fat as a pig. Don't spoil your dinner.'

Mary grinned. 'I'm a natural pig. Anyhow, you don't need to worry. You've got good bones and if you put on another stone you'd look gorgeous. I'd look like a barrel. I saw Della this morning. She's not been over because she's doing a voluntary job at the hospital. She says she wants to do something useful.'

Ann managed to cover her astonishment. She didn't believe Della wanted to do anything other than have a good time.

Mary bathed the children and wished she

had not eaten so much because she had a violent attack of indigestion. Missing a meal and then eating too much was hardly the most sensible thing to do but at least it was only a pain and she no longer felt sickly empty.

'Mary,' Ann called, 'Nigel is on the phone. I'll come up to the children.'

'Darling,' Nigel sounded harassed. 'I'm sorry but I won't be home until late. We've an emergency appendicitis and it's pretty bad. I've rung Dad and I'll get a taxi when I can leave.'

'All right, darling, if you are very late I'll go to bed.'

'Bless you, my sweet. What a thing it is to have an understanding wife.'

She didn't feel as understanding as she sounded and she was angry with herself. A doctor's wife must get used to this sort of thing. It wasn't like being married to Barry who had regular hours and she must learn to accept it. She had wanted to tell him this evening that she thought she was pregnant but it would have to wait. The indigestion wasn't helping. Now she would have to eat her dinner or Dad and Ann would worry. Why had she been such a fool. So often in the first weeks of pregnancy there was sickness and digestive troubles although she hadn't had them with the other two.

She managed her dinner surprisingly well and was ashamed that she suddenly wished she and Nigel already had a home of their own. Ann was so good and Nigel's father a darling, but they weren't living a normal married life at all. Every married couple should start as she and Barry had. In their own home with nobody else around. But they couldn't have done that because of the children. The pain was getting worse.

'I think I shall go into town tomorrow, Ann, and do some shopping. We could take the children and have lunch out. They'd love it for a change.'

'Come to York and I'll treat you all,' said Robert, looking up from his book. 'It would be gratifying to take all the family out.'

Mary went over and gave him a hug. 'I'll never refuse an offer. I'm not even going to ask Ann if she wants to, she's looking too pleased. It's nearly ten. Goodness knows when that husband of mine will get back. Nobody knows better than I what he's like when he has a patient who needs him. I think I'll go to bed and read.'

She looked in the bathroom cabinet for something to ease the pain but could find nothing. Indigestion was something she had never had before. Perhaps if she went down to the kitchen and got a glass of hot water it would get better. Sometimes Barry used to do that. Why on earth did she keep thinking of Barry?

She could hear Ann and Robert talking and

the sound of soft music so there was little chance of anyone seeing her. Martha had gone to bed and the kitchen was spotless. Heating some water she filled a glass and sat on the edge of the table to drink it.

Was Della still down at the hospital? The thought came unbidden. Why hadn't Nigel told her? Perhaps he didn't want her to know! She remembered the look Della had given him when they met her and Paul at the Metro. Did Nigel see it, too? Why did he encourage her to work at the hospital? If only she hadn't been idiot enough to eat Martha's pastry which melted in the mouth. Her thoughts got mixed up with the pain and she made an attempt to sip more water.

Carmen came in before she had finished it and looked anxious.

'Is something wrong, madam?'

'I've overeaten and got indigestion.' Mary managed a smile. 'Don't say a word to anyone or I'll be in trouble! I'm going to bed now.'

'My mother takes orange juice with honey. She says it's very good for the stomach. Shall I bring you some up?'

She was going to refuse but the girl was so eager.

'Thank you, Carmen, perhaps it would do me good. In this heat I'm perpetually thirsty.'

She went to the bathroom and locked the door, praying that Ann wouldn't come up. The pain was much worse and she was

85

violently sick. For a while she was too exhausted to move, then she washed her face, cleaned her teeth and went to bed.

The juice which Carmen brought up was delicious. Tangy sweet with an underlying bitterness and refreshing.

'This is good, Carmen, but it's not only orange and honey, is it? There's something else.'

'There's some grapefruit, too.'

'This will have to be my regular nightcap.' She drank it gratefully and Carmen looked pleased.

Mary lay quietly, trying to will sleep to come but it eluded her. The pain had eased leaving a soreness which was the result of the sickness. If she was going to suffer with indigestion and sickness during her pregnancy it would be maddening for Nigel would fuss like an old hen and that would make her irritable. With the other two children she had felt wonderful from the start and they had been born with the minimum of trouble. She wanted other babies but she rejected the thought of illness. Damn, damn, damn! And then she was asleep, soundlessly, dreamlessly. She never heard Nigel come in and he got into bed carefully for fear of disturbing her. He was already dressed when she wakened.

'Hullo, sleepy-head!'

She stretched luxuriously, forgetting her

troubles of the day before.

'Good Lord, I slept like a top and I came to bed early, too. Is it late?'

'No, sweetie, it's only six but I must get back to the hospital as soon as possible. The appendix case is still dodgy and we've a long list today. Don't you get up. I'm not stopping for breakfast. I'll have it at the hospital. What are you doing with yourself today?'

'Ann and I are taking the children shopping and we are having lunch with a charming man.'

'O-o-oh! I've a rival. Who is it?'

'I've a good mind not to tell you for neglecting me.'

He pulled down the sheet, slapped her backside gently and then kissed her.

'Much of your cheek and I'll get rough!'

'Terror has me in its grip.' She pulled a face at him. 'It's your father. He's a darling. Nigel, do you think we could get a house soon?'

'I expect so but there isn't any hurry. Dad likes having us here and the house is far too big for him. We'll talk about it.'

She was annoyed but it was no use saying any more while he was so busy. Perhaps when Dr. March came back he would have time.

'Take care of yourself, sweetheart.' He kissed her lightly. 'I must rush.'

As he closed the door she thought it was the most unsatisfactory kiss he had ever given her and she had had no opportunity to tell him she was sure she was pregnant. She got out of bed and went to the window, hoping he would look up and wave. Della was waiting in her big sports car. Her dark hair was fastened in a neat roll at the back of her head and she looked just as she had the first time Mary had seen her. Not a young girl on the verge of womanhood but a sophisticated woman. She drew back from the window furiously angry. Why hadn't Nigel told her Della was driving him to the hospital? Didn't he want her to know? She was too angry to be reasonable. She didn't stop to think that he would hardly meet the girl outside of the house if he wanted to keep it secret.

Before she had time to calm her temper the ghastly sickness started. Her stomach revolted and she dashed to the bathroom. This time she did not stop to lock the door and when the vomiting had ended she realised that Ann was by her side.

'Here's some water, pet. Wash your face and come and lie down. I'll get you a cup of tea with lemon.'

She lay on her bed, swamped with misery and absurdly ashamed. Sipping the tea she looked at Ann and summoned a grin.

'What a dope you are.' Ann was smiling. 'Were you sick with the other two?' Mary shook her head, relieved that Ann didn't think she was ill. 'Have you told Nigel?'

'Not yet. I wanted to be sure.'

'I should tell him before he finds out for himself. I shouldn't think there is much doubt!'

'I intended to last night but there wasn't any chance. I didn't hear him come in and this morning he was off like the wind. Della gave him a lift.'

'At this time in the morning! I shouldn't have thought she was one of the world's workers but you never know what goes on in anyone's mind. Perhaps she is taking this work at the hospital more seriously than one would expect. Don't come down to breakfast. I'll tell Robert you are having a rest. Later I'll bring you up some toast. Will you feel like going out?'

'Of course. I'm better already.'

Once she had eaten some dry toast she did feel better, but Ann and Carmen wouldn't let her help with the children and there was nothing for her to do—there never did seem anything for her to do. She went out in the garden where Peter, the old gardener, was watering the canna lilies. The flaming scarlet blossoms reminded her of Della. There was the same passionate intensity about them. Why had it never struck her before?

Tante Marie came down the steps of the Grant house and walked towards her. She walked with her head up and her shoulders back, her movements light and stately. The blue cotton frock made her dark skin look rich and warm and there was a serious but gentle expression on her face. In youth she must have been lovely. Mary thought of the old man at the little white house. It was difficult to think he could be her father.

'Are you feeling better this morning, Mrs. Norton?'

So Della had told her she wasn't well yesterday. As long as she didn't say anything to Ann it didn't matter.

'Yes, I'm fine now, thank you. It was a good job Della had the morning off. I was glad to have her walk home with me.'

'The morning off?' Tante Marie raised her eyebrows.

'From the hospital.'

'Oh, yes, of course.' Mary was certain it was news to her. 'I shouldn't walk to the little beach again unless you have someone with you. That path has no protection from the sun and it can be very tiring.' Tante Marie pushed back a crisp tendril of hair from her forehead and Mary noticed the long, thin fingers, fingers that had never known rough work. 'I must get back. If I don't keep an eye on her Nina forgets the most important things.'

So Tante Marie knew nothing about Della working at the hospital. Why all the secrecy? Mary went back to the house to wait for Ann and the children. There was something going on that she didn't understand and she was not only jealous but afraid although she did not know why. It was an unreasoning, childish fear.

Tante Marie went up to her room, unlocked the drawer in which she had put the wax doll and touched it gently. Was it a lot of superstitious nonsense? Papa Dan was mixed up in this and when she was a little girl she had been afraid of his spells. As she grew older she had told herself he was a silly man but it did not stop her from being afraid. Father O'Donnell called it nonsense but a lot of clever people thought religion was nonsense, too! How could anyone know? Tante Marie had read widely and sometimes she was sure of nothing, not even herself. Last night the sight of the wax figure had filled her with terror and she had done what she thought was right. Perhaps she was a fool and Della just a lovesick girl who would try anything.

Instinctively she realised that Mary Norton was pregnant and the walk in the sun might have made her feel faint and sick but she didn't trust Papa Dan. He practised his magic and mixed his brews and it was never kindly and he adored Della and would do anything for her. If only she was like Cassy with her simple belief in good and evil.

She went down on her knees and tried to pray. 'Holy Mary, Mother of God.' Last night she had believed implicitly, this morning doubts were there once more and her thoughts wandered. If only she could appeal to Della's father but he would laugh in her face.

'You're still as big a fool as ever, Marie!'

When she closed her eyes she could picture Della's mother. Slight and beautiful with her honey-coloured skin and her great, dark eyes. How she had hated her! 'Holy Mary, Mother of God, forgive me for the hatred that dwelt in my heart!'

When she went downstairs she picked up the telephone. Yes, it was important that she spoke to Dr. Norton personally. She knew perfectly well they thought it was a white woman on the line or she might not have got through to him so easily. Gordon Grant's house-keeper would have been asked to give a message.

'This is Tante Marie, Dr. Norton.' Nigel smiled at the formality. Tante Marie had called him Nigel all his life. 'I'd like to make an appointment to see you as soon as possible.'

'What's wrong, Tante Marie? Would you like me to pop over to the house this evening?'

'No, I think I had better come to the hospital.'

As far as he knew Tante Marie had never been ill in her life, but there must be something seriously the matter with her now. She hardly ever went far from the house.

'Can you manage one o'clock? I know it's an awkward time but I will be free then.'

'Yes, that will do very nicely and thank you, Dr. Norton.'

She hadn't mentioned Della so he supposed she still knew nothing about her working at the hospital and if she was not well she probably didn't want her to know. It was easy enough to arrange she was nowhere near his office at the time. Matron would see to that if he asked her. He found Della's eagerness to do something with her life partly amusing, partly touching. It was a pity she had not stayed on in England and taken up a career seriously. On the other hand she might tire of it in a few weeks. When she had first suggested it he had talked to Matron and been extremely frank.

'She's a clever girl, Maggie, but she's never had to do anything in her life. At school she got through exams with about half the effort other children have to make and I believe she was an absolute rebel in England but even then her work didn't suffer. I've seen her reports.' He smiled. 'Goodness knows how she will take to hospital discipline. If she doesn't she will have to go but if you could see how she shapes I will be grateful. I'm very fond of her and what she needs is an incentive and this may be it.'

At the end of the first week Matron told him she was most useful and didn't seem to mind what she was given to do.

'I don't see any reason why she should not go on with the work. Goodness knows we need all the help we can get. Sister on the ward where she is helping is very pleased with her. She is bright and cheerful and the patients like her.'

'That's something. She's been rather spoilt and has never gone without a thing she wanted but this may be the making of her.' He had left it at that.

Tante Marie was shown straight into his office. Her dark grey cotton frock was quakerlike in its simplicity and her greying hair was swept back severely from her strong, good-looking face.

'Sit down, Tante Marie, and tell me what is wrong. We can't have you ill.'

She sat down and folded her brown hands over her white handbag. There was pathos in her quietness. Strange that she could look so regal and yet have an air of humility. He found himself wondering what it must have been like in the old slave days when her ancestors had been torn from their homes and taught obedience by the lash. Had one of her forebears been a chief of his tribe and yet, under the cutting whip, managed to make his persecutors feel faintly ashamed?

'I am not ill, Dr. Norton.' He wondered

why she was sticking to the formality. She had always called him by his Christian name, not in any familiar manner but with affection from his boyhood. 'I want to know what Della is doing here in the hospital and why she has said nothing to me or her father. She has been in my charge most of her life and I cannot understand it.'

'Is that all that is wrong, Tante Marie?' Nigel laughed. 'I think I can tell you the reason. She wanted to make sure she was doing the right thing before she said anything. Perhaps she was afraid that you and her father would think it a flash in the pan and she would soon tire of it. You might have laughed at her enthusiasm and there is nothing more hurtful to a youngster's self-esteem. As it is Matron is delighted with her. I am hoping that later she will take up nursing. She's clever, the right age and we need nurses so badly. I know she'll get married but it would be a good thing for her to be doing something useful in the meantime. She has great possibilities.'

Tante Marie had lost the battle before it started and she knew it. If she had had any sense she would not have bothered to see Nigel for she should have known Della would play her cards right. He believed implicitly that her only reason was to do something useful. Perhaps it was as well. While she was here, working, she could not have much time for mischief and Nigel was a doctor before anything.

'I'm sorry to have taken your time. She's been home so little in the last couple of weeks that I wondered where she was.' Tante Marie was quietly withdrawn.

'Tante Marie, you are a naughty woman.' Nigel grinned. 'You didn't know where she was and wondered if the young monkey was up to mischief. She's in perfectly safe hands—Matron's—and she brooks no naughtiness. The worst she can do is to flash her eyes at one of the doctors or the patients and they'd love it!'

Tante Marie looked at him and wondered how men could be such fools, but at least there was Matron! Perhaps Nigel's innocence was a bigger safeguard than anything. It was as well she did not know that Della had driven him home in the early hours of the morning.

It was nine o'clock that night when Della came home and she had Paul with her. Tante Marie wondered if it was a deliberate move so that she could ask no questions or to make her think she had merely spent the day with friends. Her father was not home and Tante Marie could hear the sound of pop records coming from the radiogram in the little room at the back of the house which Della used as her own sitting-room. At one time it had been her own special sanctum but Della wanted it and Della had it. She went up to the girl's bedroom and waited. It was midnight before she came up and when she saw Tante Marie she laughed.

'Now what is it? There are times, Tante Marie, when I hate you. Whenever I come in nowadays you look at me as if the devil himself was loose.'

'Perhaps he is. Why are you working at the hospital? I don't believe this story that you want to do something useful. What wickedness are you planning?'

'Don't you think it is time I did something with my life? You used to be always complaining that I did nothing. Now you complain that I am working. It wouldn't matter what I did you wouldn't like it.'

'If it is only that, but I've never known you do anything for someone else without a motive. I suppose you think you will see more of Nigel. Why are you leading Paul Lacrosse on?'

'Perhaps I will marry him.' Della was getting undressed, hanging her frock carefully on a hanger and leaving it outside the wardrobe. She put her underclothes in a linen basket. 'So you found my little doll! I discovered that this morning.' She strode over to the seated woman, her whole body taut with fury. 'What good do you think you can do? Mind your own business, you interfering old woman!' Her hand shot out and she slapped Tante Marie's face, viciously. The woman recoiled at the blow and shook her head, dazed by the unexpected onslaught, then she rose from the chair, dignity in every line of her full-breasted figure.

'I'll pray that some day you will learn the meaning of kindness, Della, but until that happens don't be surprised if some of your wickedness comes back on your own head.'

Della stood in front of her naked, her golden body like a perfect statue. Then she began to laugh, deep-throated, musical. She flung herself on the bed and rocked with her laughter. Tante Marie walked out of the room and closed the door.

Gordon Grant had come home and was sitting in his study slowly sipping a whisky and soda. He did not look up as Tante Marie came into the room. She stood for a moment looking down at him her eyes full of deep unhappiness. When she spoke her voice was very quiet, trying desperately to cover her emotion.

'You've never bothered about Della apart from never allowing her mother to have any contact with her. Now it is time you took some interest in her or you may be sorry.'

There was an open book on his lap and now he took off his eyeglasses and looked up. At one time he had been a handsome man but now his jowl was too heavy and he was running to fat.

'I'm never sorry about anything. A boy to carry on after me and I might have done something.'

'Della has brains and could have done that.'

'Rubbish! Go away and stop pestering me. I've never denied the girl anything. She can find her own way. You insisted on her being sent to school in England and much good did it do. Women are all fools. Built for one thing only.'

'And you hate them! I know! All you've ever wanted from them is sex and a son you have never had!'

CHAPTER SIX

Nigel couldn't think why Tante Marie was so disturbed about Della. The girl had always been a law unto herself but now, when she was doing something useful, the woman was clearly worried. Perhaps Della was right. Tante Marie didn't think it was correct for the daughter of Gordon Grant to work. When she had driven him home she had told him Tante Marie wouldn't like it.

'And before long you will be getting married. The old dear will arrange a gorgeous wedding, work herself to a standstill and love it.'

'Don't be silly, Nigel. I haven't any intention of getting married for years. I realise now that I was very stupid when I was in England. I was doing well and then I had to spoil it all by getting into trouble.'

'What did you do? I've never heard why you came home in such a hurry.'

'I slipped out one night and went to the pictures and then I went to the local hotel for dinner.' She giggled. 'It wasn't the first time. I used to put my hair up and look about twenty, but one night I was caught. Perhaps I would have been forgiven but I was always breaking the rules.'

She didn't tell him that she had not been alone but with the son of the local M.P. and had not come back until six in the morning. The affair had been hushed up for the sake of the school, but Della had been sent home as soon as possible.

'I hated all the rules and regulations but I did want to be a doctor.' The lie slid off her tongue so neatly she almost believed it herself.

'It's not too late, poppet. You're only a youngster.'

'No, I don't want to start again, but later I may become a nurse.' He wondered if Matron had put the idea in her head. 'You will help me, won't you, Nigel?'

'Of course I will. It's a good idea to train for something before you settle down. Mary

100

was a journalist.'

'Was she really? She's so fragile it is difficult to think of her holding down anything like that.'

'Mary's not fragile, only tiny. If she hadn't had a good constitution she would never have got over her illness. There were times when Sir Humphrey Myers didn't think she would. Had she not been making such an effort to keep the home going for her children and neglected herself she wouldn't have been so ill.'

'It must be wonderful for her to feel she has you to cope now.' It was said gently but for a moment Nigel was irritated. Did the silly child think that was why Mary had married him?

As she drove him that morning she had talked only of the hospital, asking him intelligent questions about some of the cases in the ward where she was working. He was delighted at her interest. Tante Marie would be pleased when she realised Della was in earnest.

Mary had put the children to bed, had a quick shower and was trying on a slim-fitting dress when Nigel came home. She had quite recovered from her anger and was longing to have the evening alone with him and tell him that she was pregnant. In her eagerness she forgot how little sleep he had had.

'We've had a lovely day. The children were

thrilled at having lunch with your father and were positive angels. I didn't expect you so early. Do you think we could go out to dinner?'

Nigel only wanted to relax over a meal, chat for a bit and go to bed early.

'If you've been out most of the day it would do you more good to take it easy this evening.'

'I'm feeling fine. I've led such a quiet life for so long I want to kick over the traces for once.' She was smiling happily and thinking that before long she wouldn't look so trim and mightn't want to go dining and dancing.

Nigel, usually amenable to anything she wanted, was annoyed. Didn't she realise that he had had hardly any sleep the night before? He thought she knew how hard he was working. Mary looked up and saw the irritation on his face and the spirit of fun dried up. He didn't want to take her out! Fine, then she didn't want to tell him about the baby! She was being childish and knew it. Suddenly she remembered his late night and early morning. Immediately she was sorry and about to say so when he turned away with hunched shoulders.

'If you feel like that we had better go.'

Had he said, 'Darling, I'm tired, do you mind if we go some other time?' she would have said, 'Of course not, dear, I understand.' But the churlish manner hurt and angered her.

'We'll do nothing of the sort. I merely thought it would be nice to feel I was married to you for a change instead of to a whole family. We never have any time to ourselves unless we are in bed.'

Nigel wished he had spoken more gently but her cool tones stopped him from trying to put matters right.

Ann saw the withdrawn look on her face and wondered if she was overtired. Dinner was far more silent than usual. Nigel was wondering about the new doctor who was due to arrive next week and hoping it would take some of the load off his shoulders. Dr. MacKenzie had applied for the post because he had chest trouble and needed a warmer climate. Unfortunately he was already in his late fifties but if he could cope with form filling and some of the ward work it would be a relief. Thank goodness the nursing side ran smoothly. Margaret Felling had been matron for ten years and ruled her staff with firm but gentle hands. He was glad she had given such a promising report on Della.

Nigel and Maggie were close friends and she thought that had she been fortunate enough to have a son she would have liked him to be a duplicate of Nigel Norton. She also thought that had she picked a wife for him herself she couldn't have chosen better than Mary.

He sat at the table brooding over a talk he had had with Maggie that morning.

'I'm bothered over old Mathilda Brown,' he had said.

'Why, she's getting on very well and almost ready to go home.'

'I know, the old sinner, but she doesn't want to get well yet. Would you, if, for the first time in your life, you could take a rest and have the family looking at you with something close to reverence? That woman has worked like a slave, often when she didn't know how to drag around, taking in washing for women who were as fit as fiddles. Quite apart from her body her soul is getting the cosseting it needs.'

'Sometimes, Nigel, I think you see the patients' souls more clearly than their bodies.'

'I don't know about the patients,' his blue eyes twinkled, 'but I see Dr. Thorneycroft's and it's a mean one. He wants to push old Matty out as soon as possible. He did a beautiful job of that hysterectomy but he doesn't see Matty. He wants to get rid of her so that he can do another beautiful job.'

'We need the bed.'

'I know.' Nigel had stubbed out his cigarette irritably. 'We also need more money but just now I'm thinking of Matty. While she's been here the family have been devoutly tender, her old man's actually been working, but once she is home he'll stop work and start drinking again, her married daughter will give her her children to mind and young Mandy, the one who isn't married, will land her with her two children and Matty will take in washing once more. What is the answer? Damn Dr. Thorneycroft's black soul!'

'That wouldn't sound so bad if he were white.'

'Skin, skin, what difference does it make? He's a brilliant surgeon, the best we've got, but he's small-minded and mean and he never sees a patient as a man or a woman but as a body for him to cut up for his own glorification.'

'That is not true, Nigel, and some day you will realise it. Being coloured he must be better than a white man and he knows it and so should you. Not only that, he is practical and knows how we need beds.' It was unusual for Maggie to be so severe.

The meal was finished and they went into the lounge and Nigel was still wondering what he could do about Matty. She could go home tomorrow if it was to care and comfort but that was the last thing she would get. He thought of the patient, wrinkled face, the work-worn hands and the shoulders which stooped from long hours bent over a wash tub. He almost wished she wasn't quite so well so it would give him time to work something out. What they needed was a convalescent home for cases like this. He didn't notice that the conversation was being carried on by his father and Ann.

Mary went over to the piano and ran her fingers over the keys. She wasn't a particularly good performer but there was a wealth of feeling in her fingers. She was playing a piece of Mozart while her thoughts wandered. Her fingers moved automatically. While she was playing there was no need to try and enter into a conversation. Where were Nigel's thoughts? If she had used her head she would have known he was too tired to take her out but he could have said so, not spoken as if she were a wilful child who had to be given in to. Were his thoughts with Della? Had he arranged for her to take him to the hospital tomorrow? She was seething with jealousy and hating herself for it. The girl was so damnably beautiful. Why hadn't Nigel told her she was working at the hospital? Didn't he want her to know he was seeing so much of her? Then she could be just as secretive! She wouldn't tell him about the baby.

Nigel, hearing the music, looked up and smiled. Nobody had touched the piano since his mother died and he had had no idea Mary could play. She was full of surprises. Sitting at the keyboard with the soft light of the standard lamp making a pool around her she looked young and vulnerable. His heart was suddenly tender and he wished he had more time. He would try and get away earlier tomorrow and take her out. She wasn't getting much fun and she had had a thin time. If only he hadn't been such a bad-tempered brute when he first came in.

Mary swung round on the stool and said she was going to bed. Her smile was bright but she didn't look at Nigel and he wondered if she was still angry with him.

'I'll be up soon, dear.' He spoke gently but she kept her eyes away from his. Nigel wanted to talk to his father about Matty. Often he would think of a solution to hospital problems but this time he couldn't but he did agree there was need for a convalescent home.

'Could we start a fund?'

'It's a good suggestion but Matty needs help now. The only thing I can think of is to do my best to put the fear of the Lord into that lazy family of hers and to have a talk to the priest.'

'It can't do any harm and it might help.'

Carmen had put a glass of fruit juice by the bed and Mary drank it, amused but grateful for her thoughtfulness. When Nigel came up she was lying very still and breathing deeply. He slipped into bed quietly and put a gentle arm round her. His thoughts turned again to Dr. Thorneycroft. Damn him! It didn't help that he knew a vague jealousy of those dark, skilful fingers. Sometimes he thought the man could cut, clamp and sew without needing to think at all. As if his fingers had a knowledge

107

all their own. Lord, he was getting fantastic thoughts but he knew that he could never be as successful a surgeon himself. He drifted into sleep.

The weight of his arm wakened Mary but she did not move. He was sleeping like a child and that thought alone was enough to rouse a tumult of emotions in her quiet body. He can work until after midnight, she thought, get up again before six with a cheerful smile but if I ask him to take me out he gets narked. She knew she was not being fair but she didn't care. Della could take him to and from the hospital!

When she did sleep both Della and Nigel were with her. Della was mocking her with those dark eyes while she and Nigel bent over a bed. Sometimes she was the patient struggling against Della's unwanted attentions, sometimes she was watching the two of them holding hands across a bed with eyes for no one but each other. In the morning she hated herself for the jealousy that still gripped her.

★　　　★　　　★

Della wakened early. She had the gift of being able to sleep anywhere and at any time. Two or three hours and she was as refreshed as most people after seven or eight. This morning she was on top of the world. She

108

hadn't the slightest intention of marrying Paul but he was a good 'stand in.' Stretching luxuriously she thought of his love-making. He was amazingly adept for a boy and it was the easiest thing to lie in his arms and imagine he was Nigel. It was only after the love-making, when her voluptuous young body was at rest, that he became a bore and she wanted to turn on him and tell him he was an idiot. But he was useful and he adored her. It was amusing to think how she could pull the wool over people's eyes—except Cassy and Tante Marie, but they didn't count. Of course there had been Aunt Christine but she was dead. Sometimes she wondered how much her wish had had to do with that. Uncle Robert had really thought she was broken hearted which was funny.

She slipped out of the house quietly. Cassy would be at Church praying for Papa Dan's soul. The old man was already sitting in his rocking chair outside the house. Did he ever sleep in his bed? His eyes sparkled when he saw her. How he wished she was his granddaughter—or his daughter. Cassy and Tante Marie were his only children and they were fools. What he could have taught this girl. She talked to him rapidly in the old patois and he grinned.

'So Marie found my little doll but there are other ways. I can teach you many things, child of my heart.' There were times when

Papa Dan could wax lyrical. 'Listen carefully if you want this man for your own.'

He put his gnarled old hand in his pocket and pulled out some tiny bones. He fingered them gently, lovingly passing them from one hand to the other, mumbling toothlessly like a gambler talking to his dice. Della listened to his mutterings, not certain how much she believed in his magic but conscious that it gave her a sense of elation. But she believed in his witch's brews. He knew more about plants on the island than anyone. He tossed his little bones in the air and they fell to the ground in front of him and he stared at them fixedly then, after a while, he looked up.

'Are you sure of Carmen?'

'Of course I am. She believes anything I tell her.'

'Be cautious, my child. Say less rather than more.'

'I'm not a fool.'

When she left it was with a second bottle of clear, pale yellow liquid hidden in her bathing cap. The old man watched her go, his rheumy old eyes glittering with wickedness. This was a woman he could appreciate. No fear of priests in her, just a determination to get what she wanted and he would help her. His faith in his own powers was unlimited and it was greatly helped by his daughters' fears.

★   ★   ★

Nigel was just going into the hospital as Della parked her car. She slammed the door and ran. Hearing her flying footsteps he turned and waited on the steps.

'What are you in such a hurry for? You're early.'

'It may astonish you but I can tell the time!'

'Since when?' He grinned. 'You've turned over a new leaf. Della, you know old Mathilda Brown's family, don't you? I want to see them but I haven't got my car here. Father gave me a lift. If you can run me there at lunch time I'd be grateful.'

'Of course I will. I'm finished at one but I may be needed this evening.' Her smile was as innocent as a child's.

'That's my girl but don't get too earnest. If you spend too much time here we shall have broken hearts to mend in the hospital as well as the ones you break outside.'

They walked into the hospital together, Nigel beaming with approval. The little girl next door was growing up and trying to help others. He had been feeling disgruntled. Mary had turned away from him this morning and said she wasn't getting up for breakfast because she was tired. When he asked her if she was feeling all right she had told him sharply not to be ridiculous, of course she was. He had never thought her capable of sulking, and not knowing how to deal with it was annoyed.

Mary had waited until he was gone, almost holding her breath in case sickness caught up with her and she could no longer keep her secret. She was even more determined that she would not tell him until he told her about Della. It was a childish attitude and she knew it but that made no difference in her present mood. When she heard the car go she staggered to the bathroom. Later Ann brought her tea and dry toast and she felt better. This time Ann didn't ask if she had told Nigel. She thought Mary was behaving foolishly but lots of women were touchy in the first weeks of pregnancy and the strange country and strange surroundings were probably having an effect—to say nothing of her long illness. Better not to be too sympathetic.

'Do you mind if I go to the beach with the children? I feel like a swim.'

'No, of course not. I think I'll sleep for a bit.'

But she wasn't sleepy and with the sickness past she longed for something to do. Going to the window she looked at the wide sweep of the bay with the blue sea and white sand. There weren't many houses for they all nestled in large, well-tended gardens. The island was at its best. Gay with oleanders, hibiscus, azaleas and syringa. A mixture of sweet smells tickled her nose. She could see Mandy Burrows walking round her garden apparently giving instructions to the bent old man by her side. Right at the end of the bay a white car pulled out of a drive and sped along the road to Port Roy. That was Dottie Cameron going shopping. The house next to hers was closed and shuttered, being owned by an English writer who spent only a few months a year on the island.

A little breeze stirred the leaves and gave a delicious feeling of a perfect English summer day. Suddenly she longed for England, for brisk breezes, the bustle of Oxford Street, the hum of Fleet Street, the noise of a newspaper office and the sense of expectancy that was always in the air. Now she was feeling better she longed for something to occupy her mind. The morning sickness was only a temporary thing and would soon pass. It was funny that since she had realised how much she loved Nigel they seemed to have less between them. He was so different from Barry who was gentle and quiet and understanding. Nigel was gentle with the young and the sick but she knew there was fire and passion underneath. Passion that had roused her in a way that Barry's love had never done. She doubted if Nigel would understand if she told him she was missing her work and wanted to be using her brain again. And she was missing it.

If I had married when I was eighteen instead of twenty-six, she thought, I might have been content to be just a wife and mother, but by then I had the taste for work. Barry, knowing her need, had encouraged her. Why am I thinking like this, she asked herself. Do I suddenly miss my work because I no longer feel quite so sure of Nigel's understanding or is it the other way round?

Nigel's life was so full but he never talked to her about the hospital, but perhaps that was her fault. She hadn't shown a great deal of interest in her new home apart from being friendly to those she met and lazing on the beach. No doubt he thought she was content to idle her days away.

Boston was only a small estate peopled mainly by the professional class. It stretched away from the sea for no more than half a mile almost in a triangle. The short roads were tree lined, it was beautiful and ideal for the children and that was its limit. A house in Middleton might not be so perfect but it would have its compensations. Tony would have to go there to school.

She could see Clinton Harcourt working in his garden. She had only met him a couple of times since the party but he interested her. A man in his late forties with a hint of humour in his hazel eyes. She wondered if he had independent means and, if not, what he did for a living. With a sudden urge to talk to someone outside the family she put on the coolest and prettiest frock she had and went out.

Harcourt was a gardener from the top of his head to the soles of his feet. He could spend all day working in the heat and still feel ready to go on. The fact that he had a living to earn was often an irritation although once down to work he gave it the same concentration as he did the garden. He looked at Mary with pleasure. He liked her odd, triangular little face which, for all its delicate curves, had a certain strength about it.

'This is a bright morning to have brought you walking. The question is, "Where are you going to, my pretty maid?" I've a pedantic mind and feel I should say, "To where are you going?" Silly, isn't it but I was brought up by a pedantic father.'

'The answer is simple. I'm not going anywhere. I came out because I saw you working and had an urge to interrupt you!' She could never resist being frank and Harcourt liked both that and her smile. An intelligent woman with a sense of fun, he thought, and I hope Nigel Norton appreciates her.

'It takes a lot to stop me gardening but for a smile like that I'd give up anything.'

'Oh, sir, such flattery!' Mary chuckled, always ready to respond to friendliness.

'Come round to the back veranda. It's cool

and shady and Agnes will bring us a long, cold drink while you admire my garden. I warn you that unless you go into something near rapture the drink will be snatched from your hand. My guests must admire or they go!' The twinkle in his eyes cheered her.

The back garden was a riot of colour and worthy of every bit of praise she gave. It wasn't large but the amount of energy and imagination that had been used in laying it out gave the impression of size and Harcourt was lucky because it backed against the hill where no houses would be built. At the end was a bank of many coloured rocks where tradescantia trailed in profusion and at the top a row of oleanders flaunted their delicate pink and white blossoms against a background of cedars. On either side were hedges of frangipani and jasmine. Immediately in front of the veranda was a paved court with a small pond on which pink and white water lilies lazed in the sun and beyond that a patch of roses.

'It's lovely and I don't believe there's a weed in the whole garden. How do you manage it?'

'Hard work and the help of a boy. Ah, here's Agnes.'

Agnes was big and cheerful and her plump figure seemed to ooze contentment. She was carrying a tray on which was a big glass jug full of a pink liquid and tinkling lumps of ice.

Putting it down on a wooden table she beamed at Mary.

'You getting nice and strong now, Mrs. Norton?'

There was something heartening about the friendliness in these two people that warmed Mary and she wondered why half an hour before she had been yearning for England. I'm a bad-tempered cat, she thought, and if I don't pull myself together Nigel will get sick to death of me. Agnes went back into the house. Clinton Harcourt was smiling.

'Everyone here knows everything about their neighbours as you will soon find out. I knew that Nigel had brought home a wife who was a widow with two children almost as soon as you arrived. Agnes was full of it. I also knew that you had a lovely smile and very dark grey eyes, that the children were nice and you had your first husband's sister with you. They chatter like magpies and most of it is quite without malice. Agnes knew the lot!' He did not add that Agnes also said, 'That will cook Della Grant's goose!'

'What work do you do if you work?' asked Mary without stopping to think.

'Officially I write bits and pieces for the Huahnara *Gazette*.' The smile he gave her was full of fun but his eyes were shrewd. 'I've a feeling you can keep a secret and so I will confess to my shocking occupation. I write highly colourful and very romantic serials for

117

women's magazines under the sweet name of Cecile Patterson-Hughes and don't ask me how I hit on that because I haven't the slightest idea.'

'I won't give you away.' Mary's smile was full of amusement. 'Tell me how you come to be living here.'

'Simple really. Soon after the war I discovered I could write the sort of story women seemed to like. I was living in a tiny flatlet in Fulham, saving money and there was also my gratuity. After three or four years I was cramped and fed up and thought I'd take a long holiday and find background for more stories. I gave up the flatlet, packed everything I had and came out here with the intention of staying about six months. I fell in love with the island, this place was going at a reasonable price and I've never been back. Apart from when the Devil Wind blows the climate is wonderful and somehow I've managed to keep my dark secret until now.'

Talking to Clinton Harcourt made a difference to her outlook. Here was a man who knew something of what her own way of life had been. The excitement of putting things down on paper, of seeing them in print. She talked to him of her own life in Fleet Street. They were on the same wavelength and they swapped yarns cheerfully. He fired her with eagerness to write again. She had plenty of contacts at home and there was no reason why she could not pick up the threads. The thought of her typewriter sitting idle made her feel ashamed. There was so much she could write about the island if she set her mind to it. Harcourt suggested she should meet some of the people he knew.

'I've friends who live over at Jackson and they'd love to meet you. Not wealthy ones. Just middle-class working islanders. I'm taking Agnes over to her daughter this afternoon. Why don't you come?'

Before she stopped to think of Ann and the children she said she would love to. Walking home she wondered why she had said yes so promptly. The answer came quickly and gave her no reassurance. In the last couple of weeks she had become doubtful of Nigel and she had nothing to interest her except the children and they appeared to be perfectly happy without her. For the first time in her life she had lost her sense of security and somehow she must find something to occupy her mind or she would get more and more bad tempered. Ann and the children were back from the beach and Ann was looking very pleased.

'Mr. Madison has just rung and wants me to see him this afternoon. They have decided to employ another welfare officer and he thinks I may fit the bill. Would you like to come over for the drive?'

'Oh, Ann, I am pleased. No, you go on your own. It's a wonderful opportunity and if it is what you want you will stop thinking it is time you went home.'

I shouldn't think of England as home any more, she thought, this is my home now. Ann didn't ask her where she had been and Mary said nothing about her appointment with Harcourt. The children would be perfectly all right with Carmen.

★   ★   ★

Della was waiting in her car when Nigel came out of the hospital. On the drive to Matty's home she was full of her work and Nigel explained a great deal about his work, delighted at her enthusiasm and feeling closer to 'The little girl next door' than he had ever done. Until now she had been a sweet but wilful child of whom he was extremely fond. Now they had something in common, something shared. The hospital and everything to do with it was so close to his heart.

Matty's unmarried daughter was minding her married sister's children and her own two little girls. She was pregnant again and Nigel wondered who the father was. Gloria was not exactly the faithful type! George, Matty's husband, was reclining inelegantly in a broken down armchair.

Nigel looked at the littered, dirty room and thought how different it was when Matty was around. The children were playing, happily enough, in the yard.

Without any preamble he looked at Gloria and her father and said, 'Matty will be coming home shortly and she will need rest and care. What are you going to do about it and why aren't you at work, George?'

'My back,' George answered. 'I have a great pain in it. The heavy work is too much for me.'

'And washing is too much for Matty. Gloria, you will have to do the washing and cleaning in future unless your man is going to keep you and your children.'

'Oh, him!' Gloria grinned, showing a set of snowy teeth in her dark face. 'He never has no money.'

'Then you'd better do something about it. Do you want your mother to die?'

Gloria looked slightly alarmed. 'The nurse says she is better now. Her stomach won't bleed no more. Ain't that true?'

'She is better but she must have rest. If she comes home and has to keep this place clean, she'll never leave it like this, and if on top of that she has to take in washing to keep you from starving, she will soon be ill again.'

'Me, too, I'm having another baby soon.' Gloria looked sulky.

'You don't need to tell me that. I've got

eyes. Your mother is getting old and you are young and fit and if you will go lying with men what do you expect?'

The sulky look grew. Nigel had a feeling that no amount of babies would stop Gloria lying with a man and he didn't think she was fussy as to who the man was! He doubted if she knew who had fathered her children and she was too promiscuous to care if the man could give her money.

It was then that Della began to speak in fluent patois. He had no idea what she was talking about and wished he had taken the bother to learn. It was clear that Gloria understood no more than he, but George was listening with a wary, half-scared look on his face. After a moment or two he nodded several times and Nigel saw something close to terror in his eyes and wondered what on earth Della was saying. He had had every intention of asking the village priest if he could help but he began to doubt if that would be necessary for clearly Della's words, whatever they were, were having the right effect.

'When Matty comes home we will look after her.' He nodded again, even more vigorously.

'Then that's all right and mind you do.'

Della spoke again, vehemently, and the old man replied and glanced quickly at Nigel as if to know if he understood. Nigel smiled. Let

122

the lazy old devil think he did!

'I should have learnt the patois,' he said, once they were in the car, 'but I think the wicked old man thought I knew what it was all about. To think I never realised you spoke it.'

'I'm full of surprises.' Della laughed. 'Not that it is worth learning now. Only the old people speak it.'

'What did you tell him, you young monkey? He was obviously impressed.'

'Just that if he didn't pull himself together I'd set the village priest on to him and see he didn't get absolution.'

'I intended to do much the same but I'm sure you were far more impressive.'

'Perhaps it is because they feel I am more one of them. A little bit of colour is an advantage.' No need to tell Nigel she had threatened to get Papa Dan to put a spell on George. Some of the older people were terrified of Dan and his magic.

Nigel looked at her with amusement, not sure if she was drawing attention to herself deliberately or speaking without thought. With that lovely sun-tanned, golden skin and the dark, waving hair she looked more Spanish than anything. He had always accepted her with little thought but now he looked at her critically. The broad forehead, the straight, narrow nose with flaring nostrils and the delicately curved mouth. Like a princess of some long dead tribe, he thought, and wondered how long it would be before some man carried her off. Why had he never realised before how really beautiful she was?

'Would you like me to drive you home this evening, Nigel? I can manage any time. I've finished for the rest of the day.'

'Then go home and enjoy yourself. Tony will be delighted to see you. Father is picking me up because I hope to get home early unless there are any more emergencies.'

'A doctor's wife has to be very understanding. It must be maddening to have your husband called out on a case just as you are going out or have him come home too tired to go out when you want an evening's fun.'

It was almost as if she knew how Mary had reacted and for a moment he was irritated both with her and Mary, Mary for not seeming to understand and Della for understanding too much. Not to worry. This evening he was going to take Mary out and explain. He hadn't been fair. Had he had the sense to take her in his arms and talk to her she would not have been hurt.

CHAPTER SEVEN

Ann went off for her appointment with eyes

shining and Mary watched her go with relief. It was quite ridiculous that she didn't want to tell her she was going out with Clinton Harcourt. The trip was perfectly innocent and all she wanted was a change of company, but now, thinking of her rift with Nigel, it didn't seem wise. Oh, hell, she thought, I can't spend my life waiting around!

She was beginning to realise that however much she loved Nigel, however much she wanted to have another child, her life was empty in comparison with the busy one she had led. Her mind went back to interviews with famous people, sessions at the Women's Press Club where there was always someone who did the same sort of job, where they could natter cheerfully or moan about the fact that they could never call their time their own, but at the same time feel a sense of achievement. The thrill of becoming a regular contributor, the excitement of meeting new and rising personalities, particularly if you were the first to spot them.

If only Nigel seemed to need her as he had in England. The thought rose that in England she, too, had needed him but she hadn't been desperately in love as she was now. Just needing and loving. He was the one who had carried her along on his crest of loving. Now she felt lost and lonely and was missing her own kind. After the children had rested she watched them run off with Carmen but turned away too soon to see Della follow them to the beach.

Never in her life had she had time on her hands except for the spell in hospital when she was recovering her strength. She was the only child of elderly parents who had encouraged her to make a life for herself. When they both died within a few weeks of each other she had felt the heartbreak, but had been grateful that neither had been left to mourn the other, and soon afterwards Barry had come into her life. Even when he was alive she had continued to work and with the help of a good au pair she had managed easily. After the accident, with all the responsibilities on her shoulders, it had been an uphill task. At the time she hadn't thought a great deal about it, there was too much to do to feel sorry for herself, and then she had caught that first beastly cold. She could remember sitting in the club and one of her friends saying that she looked as if she should be in bed.

'I've just got a dose of the snuffles. I've an interview with that wretched infant prodigy, Michael O'Neale. He can't possibly see me until after the show, blast him! Success has certainly gone to his head but he's brilliant all right.'

'Go home to bed as soon as you've seen him.' Elizabeth looked concerned. 'I'd take a damn stiff whisky, too.'

'What, with deadline coming up? Oh, well, it won't take long to get it in the post.'

It had taken longer than she thought because her head was aching and Michael O'Neale had kept her waiting for ages while he talked to his fans, but in the morning she had felt bitter. But it was only the beginning. The weather was cold and damp and she caught one cold after another. Bronchitis hit her suddenly and, like the fool she was, she had gone out to get an interview. Two days later she found herself in hospital fighting for her life. Once or twice she remembered Nigel's hand holding hers and pulling her back from what seemed a bottomless pit of darkness. They had grown so close and she had been so grateful. Once she was out of hospital he had spent most of his spare time with her and the children. Had he thought he was in love with her because he was lonely? Stop thinking, she told herself, you are running round in circles.

Clinton Harcourt was waiting for her on the front veranda, sitting in a deep cane chair with his legs stretched out as if he had nothing to do in the world except laze. The glass jug with the pink liquid and floating lumps of ice stood on a table with two upturned glasses.

'I thought you might like a cool drink before we start. It's getting hot.'

'Lovely!' Mary sipped the icy drink

appreciatively. 'What is it?'

'Goodness knows. Every kind of fruit Agnes can persuade juice from I should think.'

'Carmen brings me orange and grapefruit juice sweetened with honey each night and I love it.'

Clinton was right, it was much hotter this afternoon. The pleasant breeze had died down completely. Agnes was looking prim in a dark cotton frock and white gloves. She was carrying a big brown paper parcel. Clinton smiled.

'Agnes has been working all the hours that are sent making clothes for her daughter. She's going to England next week to start nursing.'

Jackson was a small town on the west of the island where there was a canning factory which also produced mineral waters, a small firm that specialised in locally made fibre mattresses and pillows and a shoe factory. It was the nearest approach to an industrial area that Huahnara possessed. Clinton talked almost without stopping all the way.

'There's a growing tourist trade on Huahnara. Wealthy Americans have been buying land and there are now some good and attractive hotels although too expensive and too American for most of us but it isn't the answer to economic independence. There are too many imports needed and not enough exports. I'm going to take you to see Billy Jamieson who is a special friend of mine. He's married to an island girl and is full of schemes but, unfortunately, hasn't enough money to carry them all out yet. He's crazy about encouraging all the old arts and crafts but can only afford to do it in a small way. He's got a shed which he calls his studio and where he employs half a dozen people. He's a carver and produces little animals and figures which sell well during the season. A couple of his workers do weaving and one is a coming sculptor. His wife has a room where she teaches embroidery and they've a couple of basket makers. Bill wants to start a factory where they could produce the more easily saleable things in quantity.'

'I didn't realise the island economy was so shaky.'

'You haven't looked around much, have you?'

'No, but I will.'

'As a feature writer you should find plenty to interest you here. The island may not have a very long history but it's an intriguing one and the conditions should be written about. So far nobody has bothered about it except a brief history by an ex-governor. I'm sure it could be done.'

'Why don't you?'

'I'm not a feature writer!' He grinned. 'Candidly I don't want to. Too lazy.'

'So you are trying to push me around!' She burst out laughing and from the back seat came a chuckle.

'He's a great pusher!' Mary looked back at Agnes and smiled.

'Don't tell me he pushes you.'

'No, but he pushed my Susan and made her study hard. She wouldn't have got through her English without him.'

The car stopped in a narrow back street and a tall girl came running out of a small house.

'I began to think you weren't coming, Mother. Auntie isn't back from work yet. Hullo, Mr. Harcourt, how are you?' Then she saw the stranger and was immediately shy.

'Susan, the pride and hope of the family, Mary. This is Mrs. Norton, Dr. Nigel's wife, Susan.'

The girl held out her hand, her face wreathed in smiles.

'I am pleased to meet you Mrs. Norton. Dr. Nigel is a wonderful doctor.' The warmth in her voice was good to hear.

'Good luck in your nursing, Susan, and I do hope you enjoy England. Have you friends there?'

'Oh, yes, there are a lot of people from Huahnara studying and working.'

'That's good, but I would like to give you a letter to a friend of mine. She's warm and kindly and would make you very welcome.'

'That is good of you and I am very grateful. Will you come in?'

'Not now,' Clinton put in. 'I'm taking Mrs. Norton to see the Jamiesons.'

'You'll like them,' the girl answered. 'They're nice.'

'Is Agnes a widow?' Mary asked as they drove off.

Clinton looked at her and there was a certain amount of amusement in his eyes, as if he wondered what effect his words would have on her.

'Lord, no, she's never been married. It isn't looked on as too big a slip from grace here if a woman has a baby without a wedding ring. It happens too often although not as much as it used to do. We are getting sophisticated and marriage is becoming more and more a status symbol.'

'But what happens to the women and their babies?'

'At first their parents may be furious but their rage dies and the babies are looked after by the family in most cases. The majority of women here would rather have an illegitimate child than be married without any. Here children are usually loved and cared for however poor the family. Sometimes the woman marries later and the husband takes over the child. Women don't often go on having little bastards and don't ask me why. Whether after the first mistake they become

131

virtuous or more shrewd I wouldn't know.'

'But Agnes has never married!'

'I think she is happy as she is.' He was looking straight ahead.

And that, thought Mary, is my first introduction to the difference in the attitude to morals here and at home. It was typical that she thought it was the attitude to morals rather than the morals themselves. She doubted if they were much different anywhere in the so-called civilised world.

Bill and Dorothea Jamieson were charming and their two children delightful. Dorothea was busy teaching a young girl how to make embroidered book marks. The word 'Huahnara' was embroidered down the length and at the bottom was a Negress carrying a basket on her head. The stitches were simple but the effect was colourful and attractive. An older woman was making a tablecloth, again it was simple and colourful, but over by the window another woman was putting fine and delicate stitches into white linen.

'We make a wide range. Everything from very cheap to very expensive. The expensive mainly for Americans!' Dorothea smiled showing perfect teeth gleaming white against her red lips and coffee-coloured skin. Mary wondered why anyone should get worked up about mixed marriages for Dorothea was clearly a product of several races and the result was not only beautiful but striking.

132

Bill's studio was a hectic muddle. A lad in his middle teens was chiselling at a lump of brown stone and already the features of a boy was emerging as if he was merely uncovering them from an accumulation of rubbish. There was continual chatter, a positive hum of contentment. The older Jamieson child, Sarah, was flat on her stomach on the floor with a box of cheap paints and a large sheet of paper. A clump of green which was clearly meant for trees and a sweep of blue for the sea. She looked up at Mary with a cheerful smile, her face full of character, the big, brown eyes twinkling.

'This is where we swim.' She could be no more than five but there was a bright self-assurance without any precocity.

Little Mark was hanging on to his mother's hand, the first finger of his right hand stuffed firmly in his mouth. Nobody said, 'Take your finger out of your mouth!'

'You must be longing for a cup of tea. Jean will have it ready by now.'

The living-room was sparsely furnished but comfortable and spotless. Clearly the Jamiesons could not afford luxuries. The children sat at a small table, one on either side and Sarah looked after her little brother with motherly care. It was cool and airy and a fan in the corner made a gentle buzz.

Bill talked about the island, the need for a better economy and his plan for expansion.

He was a voluble talker and what he said made sense. Dorothea's eyes seldom left his face and there was no doubt she was with him all the way. It was later that she told Mary she had spent two years in England studying design and needlework.

'Academically I was an awful flop. What brains I have are in my fingers.'

'And damn clever fingers they are,' said Bill. 'I saw you looking at the head young Luke is sculpting. He's a natural artist but I am doing my best to see he gets a scholarship to a school of art at home. I want him to widen his ideas. Although I can help he deserves more training than I am capable of giving. There's a future for that boy.'

Mary looked at her watch. It was past six.

'Oh, heavens, I didn't tell anyone I was going out. They'll all be having kittens, convinced I am ill or lost.'

'Use the phone,' said Bill, 'and put them out of their misery.'

It was Ann who answered. Mary explained briefly that she was with some friends of Clinton Harcourt and not to worry. When she heard that Nigel had been home for some time she felt a momentary sense of loss. The first time he had been home early for ages and she had to be out! Then irritation rose. So what, he had to learn at some time that she couldn't always wait and hope. He could have told her he might be home early.

134

Clinton was already on his feet. They left with promises that he would bring her again before too long.

'Why didn't you leave a message to say you were going out?' he asked.

'I didn't think we should be away so long or I would have done.'

'Never mind, blame it on me. My back's broad.' He grinned at her. 'We'll pick up Agnes and it won't take us long to get home.'

'Don't worry!' She was thoughtful. 'I've had a wonderful time and you are right, I must do some articles about the island. I know an editor who I think will take them.'

'Anything you want to know I'll be glad to tell you, if I know myself! If I don't I can always find out and anything you want to see just ask. I'll be glad to run you anywhere.'

'You've started the ink in my veins flowing but don't let me encroach on your own work.'

'It will be a pleasure.' He drove swiftly but carefully.

Mary was conscious that although the wind was blowing again it was stiflingly hot and taking out her handkerchief she mopped her face. Clinton felt the movement rather than saw it.

'Hot, isn't it? The Devil Wind is beginning to blow in earnest. Let's hope it doesn't last long for instead of cooling the air it seems to intensify the heat. It seres everything.'

Ann was deep in conversation with Robert

135

when Mary went in. There was no sign of Nigel but from upstairs she could hear Tony laughing and little squeals of delight from Judith. She wished she had told them where she was going. Like a tide sweeping over her she knew her need for Nigel's love and understanding. She must talk to him, tell him about the baby and her need to have something to occupy her mind. She had been behaving like a fool but had come to her senses at last. Robert looked up with his warm smile.

'Have you enjoyed your outing?'

'It was terribly interesting but I'm ashamed I didn't leave a message. Clinton took me to visit the Jamiesons and I forgot the time.' Her face was alight with enthusiasm.

'They're a charming couple but always so busy one hardly ever meets them socially. If anyone can give you an interest in the island, they can.'

'I've been idle long enough.' Mary's eagerness was a flame. 'Clinton thinks I should do some articles on the island and he's right. How much does anyone in England know about Huahnara unless it is to think of it as a playground for the wealthy. Never as a permanent home for some and where the economy is stretched to its limit and—!' She stopped, suddenly aware of amusement on Ann's face and astonishment on Robert's. Clearly he had never thought of her as a

136

writer.

'Oh, dear, there I go, spilling all over when I see something to write about.' She gave them a rueful smile. 'Interviews were my mainstay, but I always loved it when I had the chance to do a feature on a project and I'm dying to do one on the Jamiesons and their work. What they are trying to do is so sane and sensible and they both have vision.'

'You're right, my love, the island should be written about and I'm proud that you want to do it.' Robert was full of admiration. This was a Mary he had not suspected. 'If I can help in any way you tell me.'

'Bless you, Daddy Robert, for that bit of encouragement.' The world took on a rosier hue. Perhaps Nigel, too, would be just as encouraging. She hugged her father-in-law. He held her close for a moment.

'My son has not only found himself a wonderful wife but brought the island two assets. Go along, Ann, tell her your news.'

'I've got the job and Robert has persuaded me to go on living here for a while. I've been a devil, too, and bought a little car.' Ann's green eyes were twinkling and her pleasant face bubbling with fun. 'The car is not in its first youth but the engine is good. A friend of Robert's vouched for it.'

'Ann, I'm so pleased.' Mary's earlier doubts had left her. 'I had hated the thought of you going back to England. I know how much you like it here. Tell me all about it later. I must go up to the children. It was naughty of me to stay away for so long.'

'I should sit down and take it easy.' Robert held out his cigarette case. 'Della and Nigel are with them and they sound as if they are having a good time.'

'Robert's right, poppet, relax. You can go up later.'

For a moment the biting jealousy caught Mary again then she caught hold of herself and took a cigarette from Robert.

A few minutes later Nigel came into the room with Della. Mary, super-sensitive to atmosphere, felt the tension immediately. Della, looking superbly beautiful and very happy, smiled at Mary but there was a tight line on either side of Nigel's mouth.

'Did you have a good time with Clinton Harcourt? He's rather a pet, isn't he? Where was Agnes?' Della's tones were innocent but Mary could feel an insinuation and she knew Ann did the same by the slight raising of her dark brows. Robert looked puzzled, as if he were not sure. The lines at the sides of Nigel's mouth deepened.

'I enjoyed myself immensely, thank you. Clinton was taking Agnes to see her daughter and suggested I should go and meet some friends of his.' Only a few moments before Mary had been full of warmth, now her voice was frigidly polite.

'Oh, dear,' Della was suddenly anxious and very young, 'have I said something I shouldn't?'

'Of course not, my dear,' Robert spoke quickly and affectionately, but he, too, felt the tension.

It was Nigel who set a match to Mary's anger. She had been full of ideas, longing to talk to him, to admit she had been behaving stupidly but he gave her no welcome, instead his voice was cold and disapproving.

'No doubt Mary is tired after her outing.'

'If there is one more remark about my feeling tired, as if I am a chronic invalid or a hypochondriac, I shall lose my temper completely.' She stood up, her eyes dark with sudden anger and a red flush on her fair cheeks. 'Conversation with intelligent people who are also creative is hardly likely to wear me out, particularly as I happen to be used to their kind. I am going up to have a shower and don't wait dinner for me. I'm not hungry. An atmosphere of disapproval doesn't exactly stimulate the appetite.'

She walked out of the room with her head held high but her heart was thumping painfully and she was conscious of having made a stupid exhibition of herself.

Della stood with her hands hanging limply by her sides, her great dark eyes turned to Nigel and slowly they filled with tears which spilled over.

'I'm so sorry,' she murmured, but about what she did not say.

'Don't be silly, dear.' Nigel spoke gently. 'Mary isn't angry with you.'

As if his words gave her impetus, Della turned and ran from the house. Nigel hesitated only a moment and then went after her. He caught her before she reached the gate and took her in his arms as though she were a child.

'Don't cry, poppet, it wasn't your fault. Mary hates anyone to think she might be tired and it was silly of me to say it.'

Della was sobbing on his shoulder. 'I never dreamt she was like that. How could she be so unkind? I thought she loved you.'

Nigel gave her a gentle shake. 'Now you are being stupid. Don't you ever get fed up with people repeating the same silly remark? Of course Mary and I love each other but that doesn't mean you always agree.' He put his hand under her chin and turned her face to his. 'Now trot along home and forget all about it.' He bent and kissed her and suddenly her arms were round his neck. What was intended to be one of the light kisses he had so often planted on her lips became very close to a desperately passionate one. She took her arms away quickly and her mouth withdrew from his then she gave a little sob.

'Oh, Nigel, I'm sorry!' Then she was gone.

Nigel stood in the dim garden and stared after her hurrying figure. Shock was uppermost. He had always thought of her with love and affection, but there had never been the slightest passion in it, and he would not have believed it if anyone had said she felt more than sisterly love for him. But that kiss, short as it had been, spelt far more. Della was no longer a child and the knowledge was almost frightening. Not for one moment did he think he was in love with her but he knew it would take little for him to desire her and that, coupled with affection could be dangerous. It was an unpleasant thought. He wiped his mouth carefully, still feeling the sweetness of her lips and faintly guilty. Only a few minutes before he had thought of her as a delightful, although rather wilful, child. Now! Better forget the sensations she had aroused. Had he seen the satisfaction on Della's face when she went to her room he would have been hurt as well as shocked.

*   *   *

It was unfortunate that when Mary went upstairs she walked straight across to the wide window of her bedroom just in time to see Della run down the path and Nigel follow her. She saw the two figures merge into one and turned away, her whole body a blaze of anger. She pulled off her clothes, dropping

141

them on the floor as if she hated every garment. Then she took a quick shower, hoping to cool her temper, longing to go in to the children but afraid to trust herself until she was calmer. What appalled her was her own conduct in front of Robert and Ann. She had stripped herself of every scrap of dignity.

The Devil Wind was not comfortable to live with. It squealed round the house, through the trees and there was a film of fine sand everywhere and even after her shower she was hot and sticky. Putting on a housecoat she went in to the children. Judith was fast asleep but Tony was lying with wide open eyes as if listening for something and there was no welcome on his round face. Mary looked down at him with a sense of loss. It was as if he was no longer hers.

'Did you have a nice time on the beach?'

'Yes, thank you.' The politeness of a child to a stranger.

She bent to kiss him but he turned away. Instantly she remembered the day he had rebelled against her authority. This was different but she had the same feeling of helplessness. The temptation to take him in her arms and ask if there was anything wrong was strong but the withdrawn look made her pause. Even a mother could never force a child's confidence and Tony did not want her. If only she knew why.

'Good night, darling.' She murmured the

words crooningly but there was no reply.

She flung herself on the big bed. The heat was even more stifling and she was utterly depressed. All her resolutions to talk to Nigel had come to nothing. Even her renewed urge to write slipped into the background at the memory of how Nigel had hurried after Della. Not since Barry's death had she felt so alone. If only Nigel had come straight upstairs to see if she was all right. She had behaved like a spoilt child and he was treating her like one, but that did not excuse the way he had run after Della. Where had all the love gone? Had it really existed? Had it been nothing more than a physical attraction that had died as soon as it was spent leaving no understanding and no sympathy? Her mind was a tumult of emotions. Tony, Nigel, Della!

*   *   *

When Nigel rejoined his father and Ann they were talking about her new post and he was certain they were merely trying to cover those awkward few minutes. He sat down and joined in, discussing the problems she might have to deal with, congratulating her on having bought a car and assuring her it was much better to go on living with them for a time rather than get a flat of her own.

Ann managed to keep her attention on the

conversation but another part of her mind was with Mary. There was an alteration in her. These sudden bursts of temper were so unlike her old self. There was something wrong between her and Nigel and she was sure Della was the cause. When she had reached home after the interview she thought Mary was on the beach with the children, but when they came in with Della and Carmen she said nothing knowing instinctively she would avoid Della if possible. Mary was quite capable of looking after herself and she had probably only gone along to Dottie Cameron for a chat and stayed longer than she intended.

Judith had been her normal little self but Tony was again difficult. When she had suggested giving him his bath he had told her quite plainly he wasn't going to let her. Della was going to put him to bed. She wished she knew what influence the girl had over him for she was sure there was something. As if that wasn't bothering enough Nigel had come in early and was obviously annoyed that Mary was not there and together he and Della had gone up with the children.

Nigel knew he had been unreasonable because Mary was not home when he came in, but he had been so eager to take her out and absurdly disappointed. Until this evening she had always been waiting for him. His anger wasn't helped by the knowledge that he could have let her know at lunch time that he would be home early unless there was an emergency. And why did she have to go with Clinton Harcourt. It annoyed him still more that Della knew and he was not so sure that her question about Agnes was altogether innocent. There were plenty of rumours but until now he had looked on it as Clinton's own business. And he liked him. He was a cheerful, friendly type, tolerant and interesting. It would not have annoyed him so much had he not known that in many ways Clinton was Mary's own type. That he was jealous he would not admit. The brief passage of words rankled and it was not helped by a feeling of guilt. He had treated Della no differently than he had always done but her response had been totally unexpected. He wanted to go up to Mary and apologise for his churlishness but the memory of Della's kiss would not leave him. He had a ridiculous feeling that if he went up to Mary straight away she would see the mark of that quick, passionate embrace.

By the time dinner was on the table he knew he could delay no longer. His father was looking at him questioningly.

I'm behaving like a fool, he told himself as he went upstairs. Anyone would think I had never kissed a girl before. But he hadn't since he had known Mary, at least not that sort of kiss which was almost an invitation. Had he thought about it he would also have realised there was experience in it.

Mary was lying with her face turned from the door and as she heard it open she closed her eyes. Nigel walked round the bed and knew she was only feigning sleep. It didn't help. Irritation, jealousy and a sense of guilt are often a spur to anger.

'Going without a meal isn't likely to do you any good. Put on your housecoat and come down to dinner.'

Mary opened her eyes. 'Are you ordering me?' Tears were painfully close and her only way of combating them was to snap.

'You know perfectly well I am not, but you were abominably rude to Della and to sulk only makes it worse.' Before the words were out he wished they had never been said but once started he couldn't stop. 'You went out without telling anyone where you were going and then got in a temper as soon as she spoke.'

'I can't win, can I? You are eternally telling me I am tired but when I come up to bed I am sulking! No doubt you managed to soothe Della's wounded feelings. I never know when you are coming home, I cool my heels waiting for you evening after evening, then when I go out and get treated like an intelligent human being I come home and have sarcastic remarks flung at me!' She had conquered her tears at the expense of her temper. 'If you were coming home early why on earth couldn't you have said so?'

'Doesn't it dawn on you that I don't know when I can get away? I'm not a bank manager with office hours. I should have thought anyone would understand that.'

'And I should have thought anyone would understand I have nothing to do. I haven't even a home of my own to run and it's beginning to bore me stiff!' She wasn't bored stiff, she was lonely and unhappy!

'What about the children? You could give them a little companionship instead of leaving them to Carmen.'

The remembrance of Tony's withdrawal made her bitter.

'Don't forget Della. She is most eager to take over.'

'Don't be a fool! Della is little more than a child herself and enjoys playing with them.' He knew it wasn't true. Della wasn't a child any longer and the thought made his anger greater.

She looked at him, longing to say what was in her mind, that she was suddenly afraid, childishly afraid that Della knew more than she would ever know, that in some way she had a hold over Tony but the thought seemed ridiculous and she couldn't say it. She had brought him into the world, he was flesh of her flesh, bone of her bone, how could a young girl come between them?

'Why didn't you tell me she was working at the hospital?' She hadn't intended to ask him but the words were out.

'For the simple reason you show no interest in my work!'

'You haven't given me much opportunity, have you?' Her voice was quiet but still angry. 'I'm sorry if I was rude to your father. Will you please apologise for me and tell him you were quite right, I was tired. Perhaps Martha would send Carmen up with a pot of tea. I'm not hungry.'

He went out of the room without answering. He was still angry but also ashamed.

Mary piled the pillows behind her and picked up a book but she couldn't read. Her head was throbbing and the wind soughed in the trees like the cry of a restless spirit and the heat was almost more than she could bear. Carmen brought up a tray with tea and toast and a glass of fruit juice. She looked at Mary anxiously.

'You feel sick?'

'No, just tired, Carmen, and I have a headache. Were the children good?' Did she imagine a wary look?

'Yes, very good.'

'They enjoy playing with Miss Grant, don't they?' She wished she could read Carmen's mind.

'Not Judith. She stays with me but Tony

likes her very much. She tells him stories.'

'That's nice. What stories?'

'I don't know.' The girl was wary but more than that, Mary thought she wanted to say something. The heavy lids dropped over the black eyes and the moment was gone. 'Do you want anything else?'

'No, thank you, Carmen. You can fetch the tray later. Thank you for remembering the juice.'

'You sure you want it?'

The girl looked anxious and Mary was eager to pacify her. 'Of course I do. It's lovely and I'm sure it does me good.'

She was asleep when Nigel came up. Her face was pale and there were dark rings under her eyes. She turned as he got into bed and, in spite of the heat, he took her in his arms feeling bitterly remorseful. Why on earth was he making such a mess of things?

Dinner had been awkward. He had found talking difficult and Ann had a worried line between her brows. Mary had changed lately or had he ever really known her? He knew perfectly well that in his eagerness to make her his wife he had carried her along on a wave of love. Had he made a mistake? He was no longer sure of himself or Mary. The island was so small. In England she had been surrounded by friends who loved her, she had her work which he knew had meant a great deal. Was she already regretting? If only he knew.

She moved away from him to the edge of the bed. Was it the heat or did she resent him? He turned away from her unhappily.

She was still asleep when he got out of bed in the morning and he was ready to leave by the time she wakened. Her eyes were heavy with sleep and she looked far more tired than she had done the evening before. Gently he kissed her goodbye. She murmured something about having a nice day but she didn't move. As soon as she heard the car start she hurried to the bathroom and this time she remembered to lock the door. The sickness was worse than ever. She didn't hear Ann rapping on the door. When at last she opened it Ann was shocked at her chalk white face and the black rings under her eyes. She managed a rueful smile.

'This baby is being a damned nuisance.' She could have said, 'It's not only that, I slept like a log but I had the most hideous nightmares.'

'And you still haven't told Nigel. You must be out of your mind. It's his as well as yours and it's not fair to let him think you are merely becoming bad tempered.' Ann's green eyes were accusing.

'He'll start fussing and I'm getting heartily sick of going from one invalid state to another.'

'Having a baby is not an invalid state and

well you know it. Plenty of women are sick during the first weeks and Nigel might give you something to help.' Ann was anxious but she was also angry. She wondered if Mary resented the baby. Gently she led her back to bed. 'I'll bring you some lemon tea and toast. That may help.'

Ann knew it wasn't only the sickness. What had been a gay, light-hearted household had suddenly become tense. Even Robert had been shaken. Fond of Della as he was last night he had been angry. Ann had seen it in his eyes when Nigel followed Della into the garden. Actually Robert was thinking of Christine's attitude towards Della in those last months before she died. Once she had said that Della was a trouble maker and he had rebuked her quietly.

'Why have you altered to her so much? She's just a girl.'

'She's not just a girl. Delilah, Lilith, I don't know. Sometimes she scares me with that look in her eyes as though she knows more than you or I will ever know. Sometimes I am sure she is laughing at me.'

'You're letting your imagination run away with you, my love.'

'Don't be too sure.'

The expression in Della's eyes as she had looked at Mary and then at Nigel had filled him with disquiet. Mary had grown so very dear. There was an essential honesty about her that warmed his heart. It was Mary Nigel should have gone to, but Della had drawn him and he was certain it was deliberate. He was afraid Christine had been right. There were depths to Della's nature which he had never seen before.

Ann carried the tray upstairs almost wishing they had never seen Nigel. Mary was lying exhausted against the pillows. The windows were wide open but the heat was terrific. If the wind got any stronger they would have to be closed and she dreaded that. She sipped the tea and tried to eat the toast but it seemed to stick in her throat. Her body felt dry although it was wet with sweat.

'How long do you think you are going to keep this from Nigel?'

'I don't know. He's always in such a hurry to get out in the mornings that he's not likely to hear me heaving my heart up. Once I've been sick I'm all right.'

'You don't look it.' Ann spoke curtly in an effort to cover her anxiety.

'Neither would you if you'd just been sick. In another half hour I'll be as right as rain.'

'What made you go with Clinton Harcourt yesterday without telling anyone?'

'If you must know I was bored to tears. There's nothing for me to do. Even Tony can do without me. I suppose it was all those weeks I was ill.' Ann had never heard her speak so resentfully. 'Clinton offered me an interest in people who work and I know I can get some articles out of it. Why shouldn't I want to use my brain? Is that so wrong?'

'Nobody said it was wrong but you went as if you didn't want anyone to know.'

'Perhaps I didn't. Nigel is always so full of the hospital he hasn't time for me. It isn't as if he really tells me anything. Just says he is busy. You'd think I was a moron.'

'You sound more like a spoilt child. Nigel is dedicated to his work as you very well know. You never expected Barry to be at your beck and call. Why expect it of Nigel?'

'Barry never expected me to be always at home waiting for him and he was always interested in me as a person. Not just someone to go to bed with.'

Ann bit back the sharp words that were on the tip of her tongue. Dear Lord, she thought, Mary has been dangerously ill and before she is really on her feet she becomes pregnant. Is it so astonishing that she should get touchy? If only she would talk to Nigel.

'I think you had better get out your typewriter,' she said. 'You're missing it.' Surely typing wouldn't hurt her and at least it would give her an interest.

'Isn't that what I've been saying?' Mary gave a glimpse of her old smile. 'Don't take any notice of me, Ann. I'm just bad tempered. It's not easy to get to my age and suddenly become a lady of leisure. Are the children all right?'

'They've gone down to the beach but there won't be any swimming. The wind has whipped up the sea.'

And Della has gone to the hospital, Mary thought, and didn't know which was worse, to have her upsetting Tony or know she was with Nigel.

CHAPTER EIGHT

At the hospital Della was a model worker and gained praise from practically everyone except Nurse March. She didn't mind what she did from bedpan rounds to pushing trolleys. Always bright and smiling to the patients and co-operative with the staff. She worked every morning and occasionally in the evenings and if that usually corresponded with the evenings that Nigel was late nobody knew quite how it happened. It was nearly a week after the kiss in the garden that Nigel found her waiting for him in her car. That his car had gone in for an overhaul she was quite aware. Della could find out about most things. For the past few days he had been carefully avoiding her.

'Hullo, what are you doing here?' Gone was his old brotherly ease. He felt just the same affection but she wasn't a kid any longer.

'Waiting for you.' The words were so frank he was disarmed. This was again the Della he knew, or so he thought.

'That's sweet of you but I've ordered a taxi.'

'I know and I've sent it away. I must talk to you Nigel. You're angry and I hate you to be angry with me.' Her smile was utterly innocent and rather sad.

'Now you are behaving like a silly little girl.' He got in beside her, sure they were back in the old relationship.

She started up the car without another word. It wasn't until they were away from Middleton and on the open road to Boston that she spoke again and then she drew to the side of the road and stopped.

'I'm sorry about the other night, Nigel, truly I am. I didn't mean to annoy Mary about Clinton. It must be dull for her after working in Fleet Street and Clinton is interesting and she must be used to the sort of people he knows. The Bohemian type. You know, people who are creative. We must seem rather dull to her. It was silly of me to say anything.'

'There was no reason why you shouldn't mention it. It wasn't a secret.' He was curt, defensive for both himself and Mary, wishing Della would drop the subject, it was over and done with—or was it?

'Of course not. I merely meant that she

155

must miss her work and I shouldn't have reminded her. I didn't mean to make things awkward.'

'I know you didn't.' Poor kid, he was being a bear. They had always been such good friends but her words were painfully close to his own thoughts. Ever since that evening Mary had been different. Twice he had taken her into his arms and tried to make love to her but she had been unresponsive, complaining about the heat. Had he known she had seen that kiss in the garden he might have explained and healed the rift, but it was something that never entered his head. He only felt the invisible barrier that grew higher every day. The far away look in her eyes made it easier to stay late at the hospital. The loneliness of a man who wonders if he has made a hopeless mistake was with him, painful, bitter. He wanted to put his arms round Della, not because he felt any passionate longing but because he needed comfort and reassurance. He refused to remember Della's kiss, in fact he would now have told himself that it had been no more than one of the loving ones she had always given him. Any thought of a dangerous situation fled. All he needed was a little sympathy. Mary was withdrawn, Ann was up to her eyes in her new job and even his father was unlike his old self. Home was no longer the old happy place it had always been. They sat silent for a few minutes and then Della started up the car as if everything was fine.

'Then that's all right. I could not help feeling unhappy. I'm afraid Mary thinks I'm a spoilt brat.'

'Not if she could see how hard you are working.' Only this morning Maggie had praised her and said how well she could handle the old patients. 'Matron says you get on well with the old patients.'

'Being able to speak patois is a help. Very few of the youngsters understand it.'

He didn't tell her all the conversation.

'I wish Nurse March didn't object to having her around,' Matron had said. 'The nurses are really over-worked and yet she seems to resent Della doing the jobs she would have to do herself.'

'It could be jealousy,' he had answered. 'Della hasn't got to work. She could walk out at any time.' He felt a certain amount of sympathy for Nurse March who was not only plain but couldn't afford to make the most of her looks. Della needed nothing to enhance her beauty.

She stopped the car outside the Norton house, knowing when she had said enough. Mary saw Nigel get out of the car and went over to the piano. She was playing a stormy passage from Chopin when he came into the room but she stopped instantly.

'Have you had your dinner?'

157

'Yes, thank you,' he answered.

With Della, she thought, and was instantly shaken by jealousy. She turned back to the keyboard. If only she could talk to him, ask him what had come between them but she could find no words. And what was the use? To her it seemed that all thoughts led to Della. Tony was driving her crazy with his bad temper, getting more and more difficult to handle and she was beginning to long for him to start school. Now Ann was at work there was no one to relieve the strain and the morning sickness was getting worse. This evening Ann and Robert were out and it should have been an opportunity to clear the air but Mary could no longer make a move. Nigel slumped in a chair and Mary went on playing as if he were not there. The very violence of the music disturbed Nigel still more.

Carmen didn't take the children to the beach now but up to the cluster of trees away from the lashing sea and blowing sand and Mary never went with them. In the mornings she was too washed out after the sickness and she knew Della was with them in the afternoons. Not for anything would she let her see the difficulty she was having with Tony. Not only was she feeling the effects of the heat but the nervous strain of keeping Tony's naughtiness to herself. He was her son, not Nigel's, and she was ashamed of her inability to control him. The thought that Della was at the bottom of it nagged at her continually but what could she do? If she told Nigel he would immediately rush to Della's defence and be convinced she had never been a capable mother. He had not known Tony before her illness, had never seen how easily she coped with a lively little boy.

Her whole life seemed teeming with difficulties and she was afraid that part of it was her own fault. Jealousy was something she had never known before and she wasn't sure which she hated most, herself or the girl who was causing it. Am I naturally jealous, she asked herself? She could not answer for she had never had cause before. Her parents had adored her and she had been the only woman in Barry's rather austere life. Her fingers crashed on the final chord and she stood up. Sweat was running between her breasts and there were beads of moisture on her forehead. She longed to take out her handkerchief and mop her face but if she did Nigel would think she didn't feel well.

'I'll have a shower and go up to bed. It's after ten.'

'O.K. I'll be up later.' Nigel kept anxiety out of his voice but he yearned to ask her if she was feeling all right. She didn't look it. She was white as paper and seemed thinner. All his instincts were to cosset her, to find out what was wrong but if he did it might

159

precipitate a burst of temper. In the last month she had altered almost out of recognition. She appeared to take no interest in Tony at all. He knew that she didn't go out with the children and never put Tony to bed, Carmen had let that little cat out of the bag, and to him she was either cool or irritable. Yesterday she had again been out with Harcourt. She had been frank about it but it hurt just the same. He was afraid and his fear made him unpardonably surly unless Ann or Robert were there and then he was meticulously polite.

The following morning Mary was even more sick and she thanked her lucky stars that Ann was out of the house. She sat on the stool in the bathroom and the walls seemed to be closing in on her. She put her head between her knees and gradually the room came back to normal. It wasn't only the sickness but she was getting so many attacks of pain, not unbearable but nagging. She relaxed for a while on the bed and then spent a couple of hours at her typewriter. When she read what she had written she tore it up in disgust, knowing it was second-rate. Unless she did a great deal better she would never sell.

Limp and near despairing she stared at her typewriter resentfully. Even the satisfaction of using words was denied her. Was it true this burning Devil Wind entered into your

160

body and brought to light demons you never knew existed? The thought was frightening. Dear God, she thought, I'm not behaving a bit like me. I've always been a rational woman but now I'm letting my imagination run away with me and it's a blasted pity I can't seem to use it on paper. Life has become difficult and instead of trying to improve things I shy away from my own son or lose my temper.

Looking out of the window she suddenly realised that the wind had changed and the sea was comparatively calm. Perhaps, by this afternoon, it would be calmer still. It's high time I pulled myself together, she thought, and this afternoon, Della or no Della, I'll go down to the beach and play with the children.

It was no use trying to disguise from herself the fact that she was beginning to look ill. A spot of rouge gave her pale cheeks a more healthy glow. It was a definite improvement and made her look almost pretty.

By the time she reached the beach the sea lay almost unruffled and she stared at it in wonder. Had the Devil Wind gone for good? The heat was as intense as ever and in a few minutes Mary wished she had stayed on the veranda. Carmen was playing with Judith but Tony was in the water with Della. Watching her graceful movements Mary was filled with an envy that was nothing short of childish. Seeing Mary Della spoke to Tony and they both came out of the water, Tony with obvious reluctance.

Della threw herself down on her flat stomach near Mary and smiled cheerfully.

'How nice to see you down here. I began to think you didn't like it.'

'I've been busy.'

'Are you going to write a book about the island? You must miss your work.' She did not wait for Mary to answer. 'Tony is a natural swimmer and a joy to teach.'

Tony had not looked at his mother. Stolidly he began to dig in the sand as if she was a stranger. Mary had an urge to shout at him, 'I'm your mother, why don't you look at me?' Instead she carried on a conversation with Della about the work she was doing at the hospital. Della spoke confidently, as if she knew the inner workings but Nigel's name was not mentioned by either of them and Mary felt it was a conspiracy of silence, as if by speaking of him there would be an explosion.

Della got to her feet. 'I'd better go and have another dip to wash off some of the sand or I shall be late.'

'And I must take the children up for their tea. Come along, you two.'

'I'm not coming,' said Tony, 'I'm going to have another swim with Della.'

Mary glanced at Della, grateful for the shady hat which hid the anger in her eyes.

Della made no attempt to cover the amused triumph in hers. Had she said, 'You can't do anything with him, he's more mine than yours,' it could not have been plainer. Somehow Mary controlled the rage which was rising.

'All right, but come straight in when Della is ready.' She was certain Della was disappointed that she kept her temper.

Judith was already eating her tea when Tony came in. She was an easy child and she and her brother had always been happy in each other's company but now there was distinct antagonism. Tony sat at the table with an ugly expression on his round face.

'You're a coward,' he said 'You're afraid of the water. You'll never be able to swim like I can.'

Judith stared at him, her bright eyes round and defensive and probably understanding the contemptuous manner rather than the words. Her lower lip rolled out.

'I don't want to.'

'Baby!' There was something quite unnatural in the way he looked at her. It wasn't Tony. 'You're not really my sister at all. I wouldn't have you.'

'Tony, what on earth has got into you?' Mary saw the strange expression on his face almost unbelievingly. This wasn't Tony, not the child she had brought into the world. 'You know Judith is your sister and you love her.'

As if he knew he had said too much he looked down at his plate and picked up a piece of bread and butter and began to eat as if he had not heard.

'Tony, tell Judith you are sorry for being so unkind.' Mary knew she was trying to get a grip on herself, almost pleading with him to refute what she had seen in his eyes. The boy ignored her.

'Tony, did you hear what I said?' Her voice rose a little higher. 'Say you are sorry at once!'

'I'm not going to.'

For a little while the Devil Wind had stopped blowing but Mary felt as if it had left behind a race of devils in herself and her son. This was not Tony but a changeling with none of her own child's laughing mischief but reasonable obedience. The hunched shoulders, the sullen look, all roused a fury inside her but it was not only that, it was the memory of the triumphant amusement in Della's dark eyes. Tony would do as he was told or suffer the consequences. Judith and Carmen were watching her.

'Tony, do what I say at once.'

'No.' He went on eating.

In a desperate attempt to keep her temper within bounds she managed a smile.

'Come along, son, don't be silly. Tell Judith you are sorry.'

'No.'

Mary's temper gave way completely. Catching the child by an arm she pulled him from his chair and with him kicking and screaming, 'No, no, I won't,' she dragged him upstairs and into his room. Flinging him on to his bed she pulled down his short pants and smacked him, bitter anger in her face. Nigel came into the room and caught her hand and his voice was harsh.

'Is this the way you believe in bringing up children?' He held her wrist in a grip like iron. 'Tony, stay where you are. I'll deal with you later.'

Mary, exhausted with the effort of bringing Tony upstairs, her anger spent, went with Nigel's hand still holding her wrist painfully. More than anything she was ashamed. If only Nigel would ask her what was wrong and show a little sympathy she would open her heart and tell him everything. Her misery, Tony's strangeness, which was getting more and more evident, her jealousy and the fact that she was pregnant. He did nothing of the sort.

'If that is your method of dealing with children I think it is time you left their training to someone else. My God, haven't you any idea that they need love and understanding?'

She stared at him, hardly able to believe her ears. Didn't he know how much she loved her children? Was he so blind? Her anger against Tony had gone but now it rose against Nigel.

'He happens to be my child and he behaved like a little demon and I will not let him do as he likes.'

'So, having left him to his own devices for weeks you now decide he is out of hand.'

'He was openly disobedient.' It was useless trying to explain.

'And instead of being patient you think you can beat him into doing what you want. Ann had no trouble with him while he was in her charge.'

'Neither did I until your sweet little friend next door began to encourage him in disobedience.' As soon as the words were out she knew she had been a fool to say them. Why hadn't she used her head instead of her unruly heart?

'And because a kind-hearted girl is willing to give up her time to play with a child whose mother is uninterested in him you lay the blame at her door. As far as I can gather you hardly spend any time with the children. Haven't you any sense of fair play?'

'Have you? It seems you even make enquiries as to how much time I am with my own children. Would you like me to give you a minute by minute account of how I spend my days?'

Ever since she had been pregnant coldness

had lain between them like a blanket but now it was gone and there was a torrent of anger in both of them. They accused each other with childish insistence on trivialities. Mary that Nigel had brought her to a strange country and left her with nothing to interest her and nothing to do and not even a home of her own, which, she added bitterly, she had given up for him. Nigel that Mary had been willing enough to come but now she was here all she did was to be sorry for herself, neglect her children, prefer the company of other people to his and then be wickedly unreasonable to her own son. Neither went anywhere near the real truth and, perhaps because they each had a feeling of guilt, neither would give an inch.

'I'm going in to see Tony before I go back to the hospital but don't be afraid I shall do anything to undermine your authority.' His words were heavy with sarcasm.

'Perhaps you had better fetch Della since you think she understands him so much better than I.'

'Della is driving me back to the hospital. You forget she does an extremely useful job. I don't know when I shall be home.'

He strode out of the room wondering why he had said such a thing. In the first place he had had no intention of going back to the hospital. He had come home early with the intention of talking to Mary, of reaching some sort of understanding, now it was farther

167

away than ever. He hadn't even bothered to find out what Tony had done to make her so angry. As for Della driving him, that had been nothing but stupid retaliation because he was hurt.

The boy was lying with wide open eyes staring up at the ceiling. How much he had heard of the bitter words he and Mary had flung at each other there was no way of telling and Nigel knew they were more likely to cause harm than a spanking and his sense of guilt grew. Mary had clearly been in an overwrought and highly emotional state but he should have known better.

'You should be asleep.' Nigel spoke gently, seeking to undo the mischief.

'I'm not sleepy.' There was a strange look in the child's eyes, puzzled and half frightened.

Nigel sat on the side of the bed. He could hear Carmen talking to little Judith in the next room. Was she upset, too? Why on earth hadn't he tried to find out what had caused the scene?

'So you've been a very naughty boy.'

'Yes.' Tony spoke flatly and turned his eyes away.

'Why?'

'I don't know. I wanted to be.'

'Tony, your Mummy has been ill. You're getting a big boy and will soon be going to school. You've got to learn to do as you are told. We all have to.'

'You, too?'

'Yes, of course. Now be a good boy and go to sleep and behave yourself tomorrow or I shall be angry.' He bent and kissed him. Suddenly Tony flung his arms round his neck and held him tight.

'I'm afraid,' he whispered.

'What about?' For one awful moment Nigel was afraid, too, afraid the child's fears were of his mother. 'Tony, why are you afraid?'

'Of the devil that hides in the cave. It comes out when the wind blows.' The words were out and there was sheer terror in the round eyes.

'Who on earth has been telling you such nonsense? There's no devil in any cave. Who said there was? Was it Carmen?'

Tony stared at him but he didn't answer. Nigel was furious. These girls and their silly stories. His anger against Mary rose again. If she hadn't left the children so much this wouldn't have happened.

'Now put all that nonsense out of your head. There are no devils, I promise you.' He stroked the boy's head but asked no more questions. He would deal with Carmen himself.

She was pulling the sheet over a drowsy eyed Judith. Nigel kissed the child, suddenly seeing an astonishing likeness to her mother. She gave him a sleepy smile.

'Carmen, I want to speak to you downstairs.' A few minutes later the girl joined him in the hall.

'Carmen, what is this nonsense you've been telling Tony about a devil in a cave?'

She stared at him out of wide and frightened black eyes.

'I tell him nothing, sir.'

The fear convinced him she was lying.

'Carmen, if you ever say one more word to frighten that child I'll send you packing and see you get no other work with children. Do you understand?'

'Yes, sir!' The words were no more than a whisper and he saw a big tear roll down her cheek and drop to the floor. He heard his father's car turn into the drive. The last person he wanted to see at this moment. He went into the kitchen where Martha was preparing dinner.

'Martha, my wife is not feeling well. Will you send Carmen up with something light for her?'

Martha grunted. She, too, could feel the disturbed atmosphere.

'You going out again?'

'I've got to go back to the hospital.'

'Rubbish!' She spoke with the familiarity of long service. 'Time you spent more time at home.'

Nigel let himself out of the side door. It was time Martha learnt to mind her own business.

Paul had just rung to ask if Della would go out. He was seeing less and less of her and he was hurt beyond endurance. As Nigel strode into the hall she murmured, 'I'm sorry but I'm working this evening.'

'Which of your swains was that? Paul?'

'No, it was only Flo Turner. She wanted me to go to a party and I know her parties. Utterly boring.'

'I didn't know you were going to the hospital.'

'I'm not, really.' She giggled. 'That was naughty of me but I wanted an excuse.'

'Then you can be an angel and drive me. I want to see old Joe Bergasset. He had his operation this morning and he's a pretty sick man and my car won't be ready until the morning.' He could have borrowed his father's or Ann's or not gone at all and now he hoped Della would say she was going somewhere else.

'I'd love to. It will be nice to have something useful to do. This house is like a morgue but even that is better than one of Flo's parties.'

When they reached the hospital Della said, 'Will you be long? If not I'll wait. I've nothing else to do.' She looked dejected.

'No, I won't be long. Half an hour at most.'

Old Joe was sleeping peacefully. Nurse

171

March came into the ward and the look she gave him was not friendly and he wondered why. But it was the end of the day and she was probably tired. Matron was in her office going through a pile of case cards.

'Maggie, you work too hard.'

'The same to you.' Her eyes twinkled. 'What are you doing back here? I thought you were going to take a much needed evening off.'

'I wanted to see how old Joe Bergasset was doing. I needn't have worried. He's sleeping like a baby.'

'Of course he is. He's as strong as a horse. Is Mary with you? If she is do bring her in for coffee.'

'No, she's not too well. I think this confounded heat is upsetting her. I'll be glad when the temperature drops. Everyone is getting touchy. Even Nurse March is without her usual smile.'

'She does seem off colour.' Maggie looked worried. 'She's a wonderful nurse but lately she snaps and Sister Davis isn't very happy about her.' Suddenly she grinned. 'I shall begin to think there is some truth in the story of the devil in the south wind. Even old Sarah Joseph has been cantankerous and she's usually so sweet tempered.'

'Been in hospital too long. Wish we could get her home but how could her daughter cope. Bad enough having to earn a living for

172

that brood of children without looking after a bed-ridden old mother.'

'Things are looking up a bit there. She tells me her husband has a job in a factory in Birmingham now and is sending her money regularly. If it wasn't for her mother I think she would join him as soon as she can get the money together.'

'Perhaps she will before long. Sarah won't last much longer. Let's hope that by the time Sarah is dead and the daughter has raised money enough for the fares her husband hasn't picked up another woman.'

'Why so cynical? I've got great faith in Arnold. He's not only hard working but a deeply Christian man. I thought you liked him.'

'So I do but human nature, my dear Maggie, is unpredictable, or perhaps the devil in the wind has got me, too!'

'Well, you'd better get rid of it! Give my love to Mary and tell her it is time she paid me a visit. She'd love to walk round the hospital and see the veneration the patients give her lord and master. I do hope she is better tomorrow. You're a lucky man, Nigel, Mary is one of the sweetest women I've met and not sickly sweet, either. Character and sweetness together are a fine mixture.'

'Thanks, Maggie.' He walked out of the hospital wondering what Maggie would have thought had she known why he was not at home.

Della was sitting with her arms folded on the wheel. She had watched Nurse March leave the hospital a few minutes before. Poor Nurse March, carrying a torch for Paul and knowing she was waiting for Nigel. It was funny. She started up the car as soon as she saw Nigel. Her quietness touched him. Gordon Grant gave his daughter everything money could buy and then washed his hands of her. What she needed was a husband and a home of her own. A man who would give her love and security. Poor child. A mother who had deserted her and a father who was indifferent. Thank goodness she had Tante Marie.

'What's happened to Paul these days? Don't tell me you've turned him down. He's a nice boy.'

'Don't talk nonsense, Nigel. I could never marry Paul and I realised it was unfair to keep going around with him.' The statement was safe. When they did meet they had their own quiet rendezvous. She wasn't giving him up altogether yet but she knew how to handle him. This evening she knew Nigel was frustrated and unhappy and she was certain the time was not far off when he would turn to her.

'How is Mary this evening? She was on the beach this afternoon. Do you think she is beginning to like Huahnara any better?'

'What makes you think she doesn't like it?' A wave of anger caught him. So he had been right. Mary didn't like it but hadn't the courage to tell him.

'Oh, don't think she has complained, Nigel, it is just a feeling I have. She seems restless, as if she doesn't know what to do with herself. I expect she misses her work and if you've never had to look after children they can be trying. Judith and Tony are sweet kids but Tony is a boy and full of mischief, bless him.'

He wished Mary had shown as much sympathy. Loyalty prevented him from saying anything.

'Mary's not too well. I think she finds the heat trying. Martha was taking her dinner up. Della, drive out to Marisha. We can have a bite at the hotel. I want to talk to you about Carmen. I'm afraid we'll have to get someone else for the children.'

It was a spur of the moment suggestion because he did not want to go home yet and felt the need of sympathy. Had he known the outcome he would have pulled the wheel round himself even if the car had overturned. It wasn't until they were sitting at a table for two that he realised it was a foolish thing to do.

Della enjoyed her meal but Nigel hardly ate. There was no one there he knew but someone might know him. However innocent it would not look good for he was a well-known figure and everyone knew he was recently married. Trying to make it casual he talked about Carmen.

'Tony was really scared, poor child. You know the stupid story about a devil that dwells in a cave and will cart boys off with him if they don't do as they are told by whoever is a friend of the devil.'

'Did Carmen admit she had frightened him with the story?' Della was eating ice cream.

'No, but as good as. I expect she had told him she is the devil's friend and that is why he is obedient to her but openly rebels against Mary.'

'Is that what he has been doing?' She looked into his eyes, her own warm and loving. 'Poor little Tony and poor Mary. It must be upsetting her. Would you like me to talk to Carmen and find out just what she has said? I understand these girls. Probably Tony is so worked up about having to do just what she tells him that he has it out on his mother. Children are like that.'

'You sound as if you understand them.'

'Perhaps I'm not a career woman.'

The words rang a warning bell. Why did Della keep hinting that Mary was a career woman. He looked into her luminous eyes. Could Mary have said something about it? No, of course not, he was jumping to conclusions.

'If you've finished I'll call for the bill.'

'You've hardly eaten anything and I've enjoyed the meal so much. Just like old times.' Her voice was wistful. He remembered the times he had taken her out before his six months in England and no doubt she missed the fun they had had. She had always been such a good little scout, ready to fall in with anything he wanted to do. Naturally she would miss his big brother attentions. Why couldn't Mary have understood and been more friendly towards her? It would have made such a difference to her.

It was just after ten, there was no moon but stars spangled the sky. The road was good but at the highest point a rough track turned east to where a narrow path led down to a small bay much loved by tourists but hardly ever used by islanders and this was not the tourist season. As they neared the track Della stopped the car.

'Do you remember how you used to bring me here for picnics when I was a little girl?'

'Yes, and what a daring little monkey you were for diving off the rocks. I used to have forty fits.'

'Could we go down there now? I've no one I can talk to but you. Things are not very happy at home and I must do something with my life. If I could talk it out perhaps I could get things more clear.'

They walked down to the bay hand in hand. Della sat in the shelter of the cliff and motioned him to her side. There was a heavy swell here and the waves dashed against the rocks.

'Remember how I used to sit here and tell you all my troubles? Tante Marie's scolding, Daddy telling me to go away and leave him alone. What silly childish troubles they were.'

He had never noticed such sadness in her voice before. Poor kid, how she must have envied the love that was poured out on him. His heart went out to her.

'Now you're a grown woman and before long Prince Charming will ride into your life and we'll be dancing at your wedding.' It sounded indescribably phony and was quite the wrong thing to say.

'I doubt it. Do you think it would be a good idea for me to go to England and train for something useful? Everything seems to have gone wrong for me of late. There's Paul. I know I've hurt him very much and I didn't mean to. I just went around with him because he was kind and I was lonely but I know now it wasn't fair. I didn't realise how serious he was. I am so sorry but I don't think he'll really understand I won't marry him while I stay here. He keeps ringing up and begging me to see him and it makes me feel ashamed because I know what it is like to be hurt. If I went away he would get over it.'

'But I thought you hated England!' He forgot that once he had said it would be the best thing she could do. Now her nearness was warm and sweet and she needed him. England was a long way away and common sense eluded him. 'Paul will get over it, dear. Why pull up your roots without counting the costs?'

'Oh, Nigel, need you ask? Everything is so different now.' She was shaken by sobs and buried her face in her hands.

His emotions were confused but he knew what she meant. Mary was between them. Dear little Della, so young and unhappy. She loved him and he had hurt her. He knew perfectly well he didn't love her as she wanted but she roused all his tenderness and he put his arms round her gently. She hid her face against his shoulder, sobbing heartbreakingly and he held her close, enjoying the vanity of being loved yet at the same time wishing he had never left the house. Her sobs diminished and he patted her shoulder.

'Come along, poppet, growing up is a painful business and sometimes we get our emotions mixed. Soon you'll wonder what all this was about. You're probably right. It would be good for you to go to England.'

She pulled away from him roughly. 'You don't really care what happens to me. I've nothing and nobody.' Her voice broke on a note that sounded like despair.

Suddenly she was on her feet and running towards the rocks where the waves were dashing themselves in fury. He looked at her flying figure, hardly realising what was happening, and then he was running after her. She was scrambling across the rocks and had almost reached the edge when he caught her and, pulling her close to his side, edged his way back.

'You little fool!' His voice was harsh with fright. 'What are you thinking of? If you had fallen in there I could never have got you out.'

'I didn't want you to.' She was sobbing hysterically.

Once they were back on the sand he shook her roughly and then held her close, far closer than he had done before. He was caught in a whirl of emotion. Her arms went round his neck, she clung to him, her strong young body pressed close to his and then their lips met. This time there was no telling himself that he imagined the passion in her kiss. He could feel every line of her body, the pressure of her firm, high breasts, the straight line of her slender thighs and legs. The invitation was there and he wanted her desperately. An urgent need to love and be loved. There was no doubt that she knew what she was doing. Offering herself with all the abandon of a woman who knew just what she wanted and the passion she was rousing. Perhaps it was

180

the desperation of his longing that brought him to his senses. Firmly he took her arms from his neck and his lips from hers. He blamed himself entirely. He was married to Mary and whatever she felt about him he loved her and owed her his loyalty.

'Come along, Della, we should have gone straight home.' He put his hand under her chin and looked into her eyes, in complete command of himself and the situation, knowing the temptation was over. 'Let's blame the devil in the wind. Some day, somewhere, you'll meet the right man and I don't want you to have any regrets.'

'As if I care about anyone else. It wouldn't matter if you were happy but I know you're not. Oh Nigel, I love you so much. We're not hurting anyone by loving each other.' Her lips trembled and she was pleading passionately.

'You're wrong Della. You can't take what you want always without payment and whatever you are thinking I love Mary. This was just a foolish moment because you were feeling lonely. Tomorrow everything will look different.'

He took her hand and led her towards the path, not seeing the fury in her face. They were both too engrossed to see the slim figure slip behind the rocks at the top of the path.

★   ★   ★

As soon as Nigel left the house Mary had gone downstairs, conscious that she must pull herself together for the sake of Ann and Robert. Whatever was between her and Nigel she must do her best to hide it until she had made up her mind what to do. She was sure now that Nigel regretted their marriage and she had no intention of tying him to her. She had enough money of her own to take the children and go home and she was grateful he knew nothing about the coming baby. If only she could get home before it was obvious. For the next few days she must pin a smile on her face and cover her heartbreak. She never asked herself if she was being fair to Nigel. She went out to the kitchen to tell Martha Nigel wouldn't be home to dinner and the dark face looked at her anxiously.

'I know, Madam, he asked me to take some dinner up to you. He said you were not feeling well.'

'I just had a bit of a headache, Martha, but I'm all right now.' She gave a quick smile. 'Young Tony was a little demon and I lost my temper. It was naughty of me. My husband thought I must be out of sorts but you know how children can rile you.'

'Children,' muttered Martha, 'they can be holy terrors! There are times when the only thing they understand is a good spanking.'

Ann came in as Mary went into the hall.

'Had a good day?' Dear Ann, so good and unselfish. Mary's smile was warm and loving. The thought of England without Ann made her heart sink but she must not give her the slightest hint that she thought of going. Not until everything was arranged.

'Yes, fine. It's an absorbing job and I really think I shall be useful.'

'I'm so glad but don't go taking too much out of yourself. Nigel has been home but had to go back to the hospital. He works far too hard.'

Ann looked at her closely. Was she being a little too bright? After dinner Mary went over to the piano and then suddenly turned to Robert.

'Does my playing annoy you, Dad? I'm not exactly brilliant.'

'No, my dear, I love it. When Nigel finds a house I shall miss it and you.'

'And when that happens I shall miss you.' But it won't happen, she thought. Nigel doesn't want a house of our own, he doesn't even want me. Soon she would be back in England and she would miss Robert. He'd been kind and gentle and made her feel like his own daughter. Concentrate on the piano, she told herself, keep away from thoughts of the future. Live the minutes as they come. The wind was howling again and they had to close the windows against the whirling sand. The room was stifling. Where was Nigel?

Had he really gone to the hospital? Della's great eyes with their look of triumph. Don't think, don't think! It was just after ten when she got up from the piano. She mopped her forehead and smiled.

'My goodness, it is hot.'

'Only a few more days at the most,' said Robert. 'Then we'll probably get a week or two of pouring rain which will cool the air and make everything lush and green. After that you can look forward to months and months of wonderful weather. You came at a bad time and this year has been much hotter than usual.'

'I'm going to call it a day. Nigel said he would be late. He's working far too hard.' She kissed Ann and Robert and wondered if she was trying to convince them or herself. But why try and convince herself. She knew he had only gone out to get away from her.

The heat was unbearable and even in her thin nightdress the sweat trickled down her thin body. Her head began to ache. If only she could slip out of the house and down to the beach where there might be a little cool air. She took a small chair and went on to the veranda. In the bright starlight the garden was inviting but in the morning light it would look drab. The hot wind had withered the flowers and dried the leaves. It looked like autumn at home and yet there was this perpetual burning heat which made her skin

184

feel harsh and her eyes ache.

She had promised Clinton she would go with him to meet some more friends of his in a couple of days. Get all the information she could while she had the opportunity. It would give her scope for a great deal of writing when she got home. Once away from here, from the ache of loving Nigel, from the devastating pain of jealousy, the words would come again. She had earned a living before for herself and the children and she could do it again. The new baby would make it just that much more difficult, that was all. It didn't matter about Della spoiling Tony for a little while. She would soon have him to herself. She wondered about Ann. If she was happy here she must persuade her to stay on. Dear Ann, she had given up enough for her already.

'I've been a selfish blighter,' she murmured the words aloud. The wind mocked them. She sat quite still. Why on earth did I marry Nigel, she asked herself. I should have known his need of me was only a passing thing. If I'd had any sense I would have given myself to him a few times and got it out of my system and his. The trouble with me is I'm a prude and look where it has landed both of us!

She heard a car in the distance and went in to the shelter of the window. Della's car stopped and Mary saw her fling her arms round Nigel's neck. She turned away, not seeing the swift way Nigel moved her arms and got out of the car. Lying quietly in the bed she prayed he would not come up yet for, in spite of her effort to work things out sensibly, she was seething with bitterness. Remembering the sleeping tablets she had had after her illness she got up and went to the drawer where they had lain for weeks. She swallowed two quickly and laid down again. She couldn't face Nigel or she might say far more than she intended.

When Nigel came up she was fast asleep.

CHAPTER NINE

When Paul reached home it was after eleven. The household was still awake, there was a cheerful buzz of conversation and popular music coming from the record player. Michael was sitting on the veranda with his girl.

'Hi, there!' He looked at his younger brother's scowling face with surprise. Paul was usually sweet tempered and easy going. 'What's bitten you?'

Paul went up to his room without answering. Half an hour later, having taken his girl home, Michael went in to him. Paul was lying on his bed in his underpants, his arms straight at his sides, his fists clenched and his eyes staring up at the ceiling. Michael looked down at him. This younger brother was specially dear.

'What's wrong, Paul?'

'What's wrong! Your precious Dr. Nigel is fooling around with my girl and don't tell me you don't believe it. I saw them down at Catta. He was making love to her.'

'What do you mean by making love?'

'Holding her in his arms and kissing her. It wasn't just friendship or big brother stuff, either.'

'Paul, I've not spoken about this before but the sooner you wake up to Della Grant the better. She twists you round her little finger, but you are not the first and won't be the last. Maybe she can look young and innocent when it pleases her, but she can handle men and get what she wants out of them. You ask Dickie Collins.'

Paul was off the bed and glaring at his brother, his fists clenched.

'Take that back. You don't know Della. She's my girl. It's that swine Norton who is causing trouble. And he's not long married!' The young face was tragic.

'If you saw Dr. Nigel fooling with Della I'll bet she engineered it. He's not that kind.'

Paul's fist shot out and caught his brother on the chin and Michael went down like a ninepin. Paul stood over him shaking with rage.

'Your saintly doctor! He's been leading

Della on for years. Pretending he was only fond of her until he was safely married to a white woman. Della wouldn't be good enough for him to marry but he's quite willing to have his fun now and take her away from me.'

Michael sat up and rubbed his chin ruefully.

'I won't say any more, Paul, except that if I hear one more word against Nigel Norton you'll have me to deal with. You'd better make a few inquiries before you get in too deep.'

He went off to bed but neither of them slept well. Michael because he was suddenly afraid for the man he admired so much. Paul, because however much he might say he was full of doubts.

*　　　*　　　*

Della went into the house quietly. She was furious with Nigel for not responding immediately to her need of him, but she was amused, too. She knew how great his temptation had been and whatever he said about loving Mary he wouldn't stand out against her for long. She loved him with all the force of her passionate nature and didn't care who she hurt in order to get him. Other men who had already been in her life didn't count. They were just interludes. For Nigel she would perjure her immortal soul. Once he was hers there would be no need of others. She could feel her firm young breasts tight against her thin dress and in her imagination they were again pressed against his hard body. Her heart pounded with triumph. Did that fool of a woman he had married think she could hold him? Papa Dan might be a witch, she didn't know, maybe his incantations had helped but she could have done it alone. Alone! Tonight had been the beginning. Tomorrow she would break down his resistance and when that happened Mary would have lost him for good. He would never go back to her once he knew how she could love. She was supremely confident of her power.

Tante Marie was sitting quietly by her bed. Della's eyes mocked her.

'What do you want, Tante Marie? Can't you ever leave me alone?'

'I'm doing nothing but wait for you. Hasn't a woman the right to wait for the child she has cared for all her life?'

'I don't need you to undress me, Tante Marie. I'm not a child any more.'

'You may be a woman in body but you are a child in mind. Where did you go with Nigel?'

'If you must know I drove him to the hospital and brought him back.'

'Della, child, don't lie to me. There is more than that.' Tante Marie's eyes were full of

189

deep unhappiness. 'I saw you stop the car, I saw you kiss him and I know that look in your eyes. I told you before, I won't have you spoiling his life, even if I have to tell him myself why you were sent home from school. If I have to tell him of Dickie Collins and all the others you've been so friendly with.'

For a moment the girl glared at her and then she began to laugh.

'Do you think he'd believe you? Especially if I told him why my mother left. Not because she was gone away with another man, that was father's yarn to save his own reputation, but because she found out that the woman who was supposed to be his housekeeper had always been his mistress, was still his mistress. I've always been glad she went. She must have been a bigger fool than you and that's saying something.' She sat on the bed and rocked with laughter.

'Do you know why I'm glad she left? Because father told me I could always have anything I wanted if I didn't open my mouth. And I've always had everything I wanted and I always will. Don't you dare interfere between Nigel and me. He's mine.'

Tante Marie looked at her taunting face. Was Nigel already her lover?

'Don't be too sure, Della.'

Tante Marie spent most of the night on her knees, sobbing hopelessly between her prayers, but there was only one person who

190

cared about her and that was Cassy and she didn't know how deep her sister's grief went.

*   *   *

When Mary wakened it was already eight-thirty. Nigel and Robert had gone but Ann came in with tea and toast. Mary was sitting up in bed looking more rested than she had done for days.

'Nigel asked me to tell you that you were sleeping so soundly he didn't want to disturb you. Darling, you're looking much better.'

'I'm feeling better.' There was a puzzled look in Mary's eyes. 'I don't feel the slightest bit sick this morning and last night I slept like a top.'

'Haven't you been sleeping well? You've never said anything.'

'It isn't so much that I haven't slept but I've been having bad dreams. Last night I just slept. What's more I'm hungry.' She looked at the bedside table. 'I didn't even drink my orange juice last night I was so tired. I'll have it before my tea.'

She didn't mention the sleeping tablets in case Ann didn't approve. She wondered if it was the sleeping tablets that had given her the dreamless night or if it was because she had made up her mind to go home.

The wind had dropped again and she spent the morning on the beach with the children.

Tony was obedient and polite but in a strangely adult manner. It was like spending the morning with a stranger. Mary no longer knew her son and the pain in her heart grew and with it a bitter hatred of the island. The brilliant happiness that had been hers for such a brief time had been swept away and she was bereft. She hated her pregnancy which was going to make life far more difficult but she could not stay. To live with Nigel, to love him and watch him drift farther and farther away was impossible. Better to stop fighting now than to go on and lose the battle in the end.

In the afternoon she was not feeling so well and blamed herself for going down to the beach, but she called a taxi and went to Port Roy.

*   *   *

Early morning surgery had been irksome and taken longer than usual and by the time Nigel had finished his visits it was lunch time. He didn't bother to eat but went straight to the hospital. One of his patients had died in the night. Just a boy of sixteen injured in a fight. It wasn't a vicious attack, just an ordinary scrap, but the boy had fallen, hit his head on a rock and fractured his skull. Such a young life to lose. His personal life, too, was taking a great deal out of him. This morning he had looked down at Mary and longed to wake her and ask her where they had gone wrong but it would have to wait until evening.

He was a mixture of unpleasant emotions. Why hadn't he realised sooner how Della felt about him and made it clear he didn't love her? Had Mary suspected all along? Was that why she had altered? Did she think he loved Della? Could they ever get back to where they had been?

In some ways he was grateful for Della's obvious invitation for it had brought him to his senses more quickly than anything else could have done. He had been telling himself for so long that she was just a child. Now the memory of her clinging kisses, the pressure of her body against his gave him the unwanted knowledge that she had had more experience than he would have believed. He tried to tell himself he was wrong but he knew he wasn't and he hated the knowledge. To him she had been a much loved child and he had wanted to keep her that way, in his heart at least.

What hurt was that he could see now that she had deliberately tried to come between himself and Mary. Was Mary also right about Tony? What a blind fool he had been. He didn't think for one moment she had any intention of going to England. It was merely an attempt to arouse his interest. In the cold light of day he could look back on the last few weeks and see every step Della had taken. He had rushed to her defence every time. How far had he driven Mary away? It was the way she had flung her arms round him outside the house that had killed his sympathy. He knew it had been done in the hope that Mary would see and it was as well she did not know the fury she had roused.

He hated himself and yet even now he found it difficult to connect the girl he thought he knew with the woman he now saw. It was as if they were two different people. What could he say to Mary? Would she understand? Dear God, he didn't know.

After weeks of rushing at the hospital there was a sudden lull. No emergencies, no casualties. A few more private patients to see and he could go home, go home and try to put things right. It was two-thirty when Della came into his office. Why was she here in the afternoon?

'I thought you went home at one?' She stood by his desk looking astonishingly lovely in the plain white coat and with her hair folded neatly at the back of her head.

'I found an excuse to stay on. I'm sorry about last night, Nigel, but I couldn't help it.' She spoke quietly but her hands were clasped tightly in front of her as if she was holding on to her emotions. 'It was wrong of me to give way like that but it's not easy to crush something that has been with you so long. I'd always thought you felt the same

194

way about me and were just waiting for me to grow up. It was silly, I know, but you'd always made so much of me.'

The pathos in her voice moved him against his better judgement. How much of this was his fault? He had always made a fuss of her but it had meant no more than brotherly affection.

'I've go to talk to you, please.' She looked young and scared.

'What's the matter, Della. You'd better sit down and tell me.' He wanted to say he was sorry she had misunderstood his affection for her but perhaps it was better not.

'I can't Nigel, not now. I'm not supposed to be here. Please see me tonight. Something has happened and I'm frightened.'

'Why not come to the house?'

'No, I can't do that. I must see you alone. Please.'

A warning bell rang but she looked distressed and he felt guilty, guilty because, however unwittingly, he had led her to think his fondness was more than it was. Again she was the kid next door appealing for help and it was difficult to refuse her. As long as she realised that was all it was but whatever the reason for her plea he must see Mary first. He could go home for a couple of hours and then come back.

'If it wasn't for the fact that I have some patients to see and I want to get home I would insist on you talking here and now.' He hoped he was making it clear. 'I'll meet you at Catta Point just after seven but I have only a few minutes to spare.'

'Thank you, Nigel, I wouldn't bother you but I need help badly.'

As soon as she had gone he knew he was making a mistake but it was done. She seemed to be on the verge of tears but what could there be to frighten her? Had she got herself into real trouble? If only on account of the past he owed it to her to help if it was possible.

He was home before five, suddenly hopeful that he could put everything right. He'd been a fool in so many ways. Encouraging Della to work at the hospital, expecting Mary to understand without explaining, blaming her without trying to get to the bottom of the trouble and above all refusing to see that Della was not a child. But this was the last time he would see her alone. There was still an element of childishness about her, but forewarned was forearmed.

Mary was out and Martha said she had ordered a taxi. His feeling of hope vanished but at least she wasn't with Harcourt. Perhaps she had gone to do some shopping. He had some tea with the children. Judith was her usual self but now he could see the difference in Tony. He was withdrawn and very quiet. Nigel looked at Carmen and she avoided his eyes. Had he accused her unjustly? Neither she nor Tony had admitted that she was the one who had told the story about the devil in the cave. Ann came in at a quarter to six.

'I think Mary's gone shopping. Martha says she called a taxi.' He gave Ann an affectionate smile. 'I shouldn't think she would be long now. The kids have had their tea like angels. I've got to dash back to the hospital but tell Mary I won't be late.'

Ann was feeling on top of the world and this morning Mary had looked a new woman.

'Righto. I'll put the children to bed. Probably Mary has gone to buy some clothes.' Perhaps she had gone to buy some maternity wear. For once Ann was untroubled about her.

Nigel left the hospital at a quarter to seven, wishing from the bottom of his heart that he had insisted Della should come to the house. Her car was standing at the top of the narrow path but there was no sign of her and he guessed she had gone down to the beach. She was sitting just where they had sat the night before and as he came towards her she got up and rushed to meet him, her arms outstretched. She flung herself against him and he had to put his arms round her shaking body to steady her.

'Now, now, what is all this about? There's no need to get into a panic. There are no dragons left on Huahnara.' It was a silly thing to say but often he had teased her in the past and said there were no dragons for him to slay in her defence. He was trying desperately to get back to the old footing although he knew it was quite useless.

She stopped shaking and stood in the shelter of his arms but now he felt an unexpected revulsion and taking his arms from her body he put his hands on her shoulders and held her away from him.

'Nigel, it's Paul. He rang me first thing this morning and told me he saw us here last night.' That much was true! 'He's threatened to kill me if I don't marry him at once. What am I going to do?'

He stood perfectly still, puzzled, thinking of Paul Lacrosse. Paul, hard-working and kind. It didn't make sense. He could imagine him striking in anger but to threaten a girl—no! If he threatened anyone it wouldn't be Della. This time she had overstretched herself. Nigel looked into her lovely face with the cold eyes of complete understanding.

'Della, you are lying. Paul would never threaten you. Me, perhaps, but not you.'

Della stared at him, eyes wide with shock. For him to tell her she was lying was incredible. She had lied to him a thousand times and he had always believed her or she thought he had. She did not know that the last kiss she had given him was the beginning of the end.

'Nigel, how could you say such a thing?'

'Because, Della, I am just beginning to see through you.' He shook her viciously. 'But why drag Paul into it? If it is to get my sympathy or make me feel protective you are wasting your time. Had it been anyone but Paul I might even have believed you, but I doubt it. Not after last night. I know now that ever since I brought Mary here you have been doing your best to come between us and I have no doubt that you have also been coming between her and Tony. The maddening thing is that I've been as blind as a bat, thinking of you as the sweet kid next door.' He shook her again and she still stared at him with wide, startled eyes but there was no fear in them.

'And you have the temerity to say you are in love with me! I suppose your next move would be to tell Mary we are lovers and make sure my marriage breaks up!' He was almost beside himself with anger.

Della wrenched herself from his grip and laughed, still utterly sure of her power.

'Nigel, can't you be honest with yourself for once. You know you love me just as I do you even if you didn't recognise it before. I expect you feel as if you should be loyal to Mary but why should you? Was it your fault that she was ill and made you sorry for her? If she hadn't tricked you into marrying her we'd be planning our wedding. As for being lovers, we would be if you weren't so scared.'

He could hardly believe his ears. She believed it, every word of it. The bright starlight showed every line of her face. The wide, smooth forehead, the big dark eyes, the high cheekbones, delicate nostrils and curving mouth. Never before had he realised her astonishing beauty and seeing it was nauseated. Underneath the loveliness was someone he didn't know. The child next door whose occasional fibs and wild exaggeration had been amusing and delightful didn't exist. This was a woman who didn't care who suffered as long as she had what she wanted. There was no childishness, just primeval instinct. His anger went, leaving a sick repugnance.

'You don't know the meaning of love, Della, only desire. I haven't anything for you and never would have had. Don't come to the hospital again and don't go near Tony or you will answer to me.' He turned away to walk up the path and she stared, disbelieving. He couldn't mean what he was saying! In a moment she held his arm.

'Nigel, you've got it all wrong. I love you, I'd do anything in the world to make you happy. I can give you so much!' She flung herself against him and held him in a passionate grip. 'You know you love me, you know you want me!'

'Don't be a fool. I neither love you nor want you.' She clung to him, her face pressed to his shoulder, then he put his hands on her wrists and pulled himself free.

'I won't give you up, I won't!' She was sobbing hysterically and for once she wasn't acting.

Suddenly, tired of the whole melodramatic business, drained even of the remnants of his old affection, Nigel slapped her face, hard. Her sobs stopped.

'You'll be sorry for that, Nigel.'

'I may but I very much doubt it.'

He strode up the path and getting into his car sat for a few moments but Della made no attempt to follow him. He wasn't afraid she would throw herself into the sea, knowing that his moments of fear the previous night had been another of Della's well-staged efforts. His greatest sensation was that he could not go to Mary until his mind was washed clean of something very near to evil. He drove without thinking and parked the car at the top of the cliffs on the north of the island beyond Marisha. Opening the hood he sat with his hands resting on the wheel. Utter weariness of spirit and body descended and he slept.

★　　　★　　　★

Della watched Nigel stride up the path and

her anger was like a hot flood but most of it was for Mary, the milk and water Englishwoman who had married him. Only a little of it was for Nigel and that was mainly because he was making her wait for his love. She was certain they would belong to each other in time but now she would make him wait, she would make him regret that slap. She turned away from the path and looked at the sea, remembering how he had run after her and pulled her back from what he thought would be a leap into the rushing water. How closely he had held her, how near they had been to consummating their love. She held the thought close.

It was nearly an hour later that she reached home. Paul was sitting on the steps.

'What do you want?' Her cold antagonism was like a knife. 'I told you I was busy.'

'Della, I had to see you. I love you so much, I want to marry you. Don't let Norton spoil things for us. He's only fooling. He doesn't love you.' The words spilled out. He got to his feet and tried to take her in his arms as if to protect her but she stepped back out of his reach and then, just as Nigel had slapped her she did the same to Paul, not once but again and again, but unlike Nigel she was smiling with amusement.

'You stupid boy! Do you think I would marry you? Nigel fool me! You're mad! Don't you know we are lovers? We'd have been

202

married by now if that woman hadn't caught him when I was silly enough to write and tell him I was having a wonderful time. It was as much my fault as anyone's but being married to her won't keep us apart.' Her imagination was enjoying full scope. 'Why, I'm going to have his child!'

Paul stared at her, his face black in the starlight while hers was like a pale ivory carving. There was a smile on her mouth and her eyes were pools of darkness.

'Dear God, how do you know it is his? It could be mine!'

'Don't be an idiot! Surely you don't think I would be fool enough to let you get me pregnant! Me, produce a kinky-headed little nigger! You're out of your mind!' The contempt shrivelled his pride, slashed him on a tender spot he hadn't known existed. Had Nigel been there he would have lashed into him in uncontrollable fury. He watched her walk up the steps to the veranda and neither of them saw Tante Marie standing at the open french window.

Paul drove his car to the headland on the other side of Boston and, leaving it in full view of any passers by, walked down to the beach and sat gazing at the water for hour after hour. Rain teemed down soaking him to the skin but he did not seem to feel it. Was Della pregnant? If so was it his child? It couldn't be Nigel's. Why was she lying? Just to get rid of him? His young heart knew the deep pain of shattered dreams.

The encounter with Paul not only amused Della but gave her a glorious sense of ascendancy. She wasn't a bit concerned about her lies or the fact that she would get found out or that they could cause any form of tragedy. All her life she had had what she wanted and she would have it now and whoever was hurt in the process was a matter of indifference. For once Tante Marie was not waiting for her and she smiled. Perhaps Tante Marie had given up the unequal struggle.

When she left the house again it was by the back way and through the garden to the cluster of trees and on to the white house. Cassy would be fast asleep by now, worn out with hard work and the fact that she was always up at five in order to go to six o'clock mass. Papa Dan only slept in cat naps and often on hot nights in his rocking chair outside the house. Cassy had long ago given up trying to persuade him to undress and go to bed like respectable people. He wakened at Della's touch and gave her a toothless grin.

'What now?'

Della stood in front of him and kept her voice low but it was full of scorn.

'I don't believe your magic is any good, Papa Dan. You can't really do what you say you can. You play with your witch's brew and your little bones but nothing happens.'

'You think so!' His grin was evil. 'But they are no longer happy, they quarrel, I know, I feel it, here.' He touched his wrinkled forehead with a gnarled hand.

'You mean somebody told you.' She looked down at him with unconcealed mockery.

'You think so? Who is there who would tell me?'

'I don't believe you, Papa Dan. You can't do a thing.'

'Don't say that, child, or you may be sorry. See!' He drew two little wax dolls from his pocket and they lay on his hand, their tiny arms were stiffly by their sides but they were joined at the ribline so that they lay across each other in the form of an X. 'Do you want them to part?'

'Of course I do, I wish she was dead. I hate her!' She went down on her knees in front of him.

There was a sudden change in the old face, he looked into Della's eyes earnestly and his own narrowed. It was as if he saw her for the first time and he was afraid.

'Be careful, child, you go too far, too quickly.' He put a hand on her thick hair and, holding it tight, tipped her face backwards so that the light from the rising moon fell full on it. 'The little dolls, the bones, the brew, all have their place but they are for fools, to frighten Cassy and Marie, the real strength is here.' Again he touched his wrinkled forehead and the wax figures dropped to the ground, unnoticed.

'And how much can you do with that? So the rest is all mumbo-jumbo, as I thought! Well, I can manage without you. Even the brew was just coloured water, I suppose.'

'No, just plants, but it is what I wish that counts.'

'Then wish her dead!' There was so much hate in the voice it seemed impossible it could have come from the lovely young face.

Papa Dan still held her hair, looking at her intently, then he closed his eyes. When he opened them they held a strange, far away expression.

'It won't work, child, there is something in the way. Love or hate, I don't know which. Don't tread on dark paths again. The doctor and his wife have gone away from me and I feel death.'

'What do you mean, you old fool? Tell me, tell me.' Her voice was a husky whisper. The old hand had fallen from her head and he seemed to sleep again for his eyes had closed. She shook him vigorously. He blinked and stared at her as if he did not know what she was talking about.

'Go away, I'm tired.' He levered himself slowly from the chair. 'Cassy is right, I'm old and it is better in bed.' He went into the house as if he did not know Della was there.

So there was no truth in his supposed

powers. Well, she'd never really believed it and she didn't need him. There were other ways of getting rid of Mary and once she had gone Nigel would need her. She turned away from the house and walked towards the trees. The first few spots of rain fell. It wasn't until she saw the dark shadows thrown by the twisted trunks that she thought of Papa Dan's words. 'Don't tread on dark paths again!' Black clouds blotted out the moon. Della walked on, supremely self-confident. Better hurry home before the storm really broke. Tomorrow she would see Mary.

CHAPTER TEN

Mary found no difficulty in booking passages for herself and the children. In less than two weeks she would be on her way home. As she put the reservations in her handbag she began to ask herself if she had been fair to anyone. She could have talked it out, come to an agreement with Nigel. She walked along blindly, part of her mind saying she had done the right thing, the sensible thing. Nigel was clearly in love with Della and it was better she should leave, with no fuss, no angry words. The other part of her mind was saying she was behaving with childish irresponsibility.

The scene on the waterfront took her

attention from herself. Big women in bright dresses with huge baskets balanced neatly on their kinky hair, grinned toothily as they exchanged remarks with idlers and workers alike. Some of the badinage was lewd in the extreme, but nobody took offence. It was all good-hearted fun. Most of the baskets were full of packages but in the morning they had held fruit and flowers from the small plantations.

Mary leant on a low wall and watched the loading of a banana boat and was appalled at how little she really knew about Huahnara and its people. Had it not been for Clinton Harcourt she would have known even less. Unexpectedly she felt a wave of regret. How could she have wasted so much time. It was as if a thin grey drop lightly dimming the transformation scene in a stage musical had lifted, showing the brilliance and beauty which had been veiled. Suddenly she saw the island with different eyes and wanted to stay, to know it better, to appreciate and love it as Clinton loved it, as Robert loved it, as the Jamiesons loved it. As Nigel loved it? She wasn't sure but deep down she felt that the place did not matter to him a great deal. His job was to cure the sick and where he did it and who the people were did not matter. Perhaps, she thought, it's our very difference which makes me love him so. No good regretting, this was a phase in her life which had been coloured brightly for a brief while only and once she was back in England she would pick up the threads of her old life again. Life was always changing. You never knew what would happen next.

The banana boat lurched violently. No, it wasn't the boat but the ground. Mary held on to the wall. The heat grew more intense. Sweat dripped from her nose, ran down between her breasts. Her clothes clung to her. She longed to mop her face but dare not loosen her grip on the wall. Wave after wave of sickness engulfed her, catching her in its grip so that what would have normally covered her with shame and confusion didn't matter. Then, when she least expected it, she slipped into a dark well of complete oblivion.

She had no idea how long she was unconscious but she wakened in a darkened room. The bed was not her own. She realised that at once because it was lumpy but the thing she was most conscious of was pain which tore at her stomach and made her groan miserably. She had no idea of time but it must be late for there was a light showing through a slightly open door and she could hear voices which she did not recognise. She tried to get to her feet but the pain caught her agonisingly and she gave a gasping cry. The door opened wide, the light was switched on and she closed her eyes against the glare of an unshielded light bulb. When she opened

209

them again there was a dark face close to hers.

'Feeling better, honey? You sure had a good sleep!' There was a pause and then she heard another note in the voice. 'You's sick!' The face receded and she heard the voice again, farther away.

'Jesus, that woman ain't drunk at all. She's sick, very sick! Bengy, you go and get the doctor, quick. Holy Mary, I thought she was sleeping off the drink.'

The pain was back and nothing mattered, nothing at all except the misery of wrenching agony which swallowed up her thoughts. There was coming and going and a dark face asking questions which meant nothing at all. She knew she was being rolled in a blanket and moved somewhere but it was all too vague to convey anything rational. Once she heard her own voice crying, 'Nigel, Nigel!' but it couldn't really be hers. There was a long interval and then a voice she thought she knew said, 'Dear God, it's Dr. Norton's wife.'

*   *   *

Once the children were tucked up in bed and there was still no sign of Mary Robert and Ann began to worry. In desperation they rang Clinton Harcourt but he said he had seen nothing of her and wondered if she had gone to see the Jamiesons. He would find out and then ring them back. A few minutes later he rang to say she had not been there but he didn't think there was any need to worry. She was a capable young woman and probably doing a little exploring. It was easy to forget time when you were interested.

'Robert, she wouldn't go off like that in a taxi and not come back without letting us know. There must be something wrong.'

'Now, now, my dear, don't start panicking. If there was an accident she would have been taken to hospital and we would have heard. No, Clinton must be right. She's doing a bit of exploring and forgotten the time.' But he, too, had a deep sense of fear. Could there have been an accident on one of the less frequented roads where it might not be discovered for hours?

'Nigel will be back soon, stop worrying!' He spoke with more confidence than he felt but Ann, knowing Mary's pregnancy and the unaccustomed sickness she had been suffering from was unable to push her fears away. But she had looked so much better this morning! She had been so different of late. Nervous, overemotional and quick tempered. Was she far more unhappy than she suspected? But however unhappy she would never do anything crazy. She was too well-balanced and rational but why had she said nothing to Nigel about the coming baby? The heat and the continual grinding of the cicadas jarred on Ann's nerves until she could have screamed. The anxiety showed clearly in her green eyes and the taut lines of her homely face.

'Ann, what is it? There's something else that's bothering you. You're worried about Nigel and Mary, aren't you?' She nodded, too afraid to put her chaotic thoughts into words. 'Can't you tell me?'

'It's—oh, dear, I'm no doubt getting worked up about nothing but Mary isn't behaving at all like herself these days and I don't really know why. It's as if something has got into her that I don't understand.'

It was getting on for eight when Margaret Felling rang and asked for Nigel.

'He isn't in yet, Maggie, is it important?'

'Yes, I'm afraid it is. He left here about an hour ago so he should be with you soon. I expect he called to see a patient on the way home but he said nothing about it. Will you ask him to come back at once. Robert, I don't want to alarm you but it's Mary. She's just been brought into the hospital and she's very ill. I can't say any more at the moment but Nigel shouldn't be long.'

He told Ann quietly and she stared at him out of frightened eyes.

'I think I'll go the hospital now. You can tell Nigel.'

'I'll leave a note and drive you there.'

Had Nigel seen Dr. Thorneycroft when

Ann and Robert arrived at the hospital he might have revised some of his ideas for Thorneycroft was more than concerned about Mary, he was deeply grieved.

'We were called soon after seven by a doctor at Port Roy. He didn't know who she was but it's a complicated story. Apparently one of the women down at the waterside saw Mrs. Norton holding onto the wall as if she was faint. Then she was violently sick and passed out. The woman thought she was drunk and she and a man got her into the woman's cottage and put her to bed where they left her to sleep it off. A long time later the woman heard a groan and went in to her and realised she was ill and called the doctor. She was haemorrhaging badly and he asked us for a bed. Did you know she was pregnant?' Ann nodded and Robert stared.

'The first thing is a transfusion. Then I want Nigel for permission to operate. There's no chance of saving the baby but we can save her.'

'Nigel should be here at any moment.' Robert patted Ann's shoulder. 'If he left the hospital before seven I can't understand why he wasn't home.'

Thorneycroft's dark face was angry. 'Why not try the Grant house and see where the girl is. He's probably with her. In the meantime his wife is more important. If you can't find him will you be willing to give permission?'

'Dr. Thorneycroft, I don't know what you are implying but I will ring the Grant house.'

'He was with her last night and if he hasn't gone straight home he is probably with her tonight and won't be the first man that little witch has got hold of. Don't worry, Mr. Norton. You son doesn't like me and I don't know that I like him, but I have no intention of talking about this. He is too good a doctor for me to wish to damage his career and I certainly do not wish to hurt his wife. I'd like to wring that girl's neck, that's all. Now will you do your best to get hold of Dr. Norton?'

Tante Marie answered the phone. Della was not at home and she did not know where Nigel was. He had not been to the house.

Robert signed the paper and then sat and held Ann's hand. It wasn't any use going in to Mary. She was unconscious. After a while Robert began to talk.

'Had you any idea this was going on, Ann?'

'If you mean something between Della and Nigel I don't think there is. I think Della has done her best to make it so but no more. I've been sure for weeks that Mary was unhappy but she has never been one to make a fuss. I think now there was more than unhappiness but I don't know what.' It was strange that what seemed important was that glass of orange juice. She told Robert how sick Mary had been each morning and how much better she had been today and then the remark about not drinking the juice overnight but having it before her tea this morning.

'Mary said she was never sick when she was having the other two and I've a feeling there is a connection. Or perhaps I'm letting my imagination run away with me.'

'I feel guilty for not seeing what was going on. I've always treated Della like a child. I must have been out of my mind.'

'Don't blame yourself, Robert, there was nothing you could have done.'

'No, I suppose not. Where on earth can Nigel be?'

* * *

A heavy drop of rain on Nigel's neck made him stir but it took several more to waken him and even then he sat on for a few more minutes. By the time he closed the sunshine roof it was pouring. Once he had closed it he mopped his head and then looked at his watch. It was getting on for midnight. Dark clouds scuttled across the sky and the rain teemed. He started up the car and called himself everything under the sun for sleeping when he should have hurried back to Mary. Now she would be asleep and he would have to wait for morning before he talked to her. The drive took far longer than usual for the roads were already bad.

Martha was sitting on a chair in the hall the

note Robert had written in her hand. She looked old and tired and her eyes were heavy with tears.

'When was this written, Martha?'

'Just after seven. Your father rang twice to know if you had come in.'

'Thank you, Martha.'

He drove to the hospital with his heart beating wildly. There was nothing in the note to give him any idea what was wrong. Robert and Ann were sitting in the waiting room and he was still holding her hand. Nigel had never seen such bitter anger on his father's face. He explained briefly what had happened, asking no questions as to where Nigel had been.

Mary was in a side ward and still deeply unconscious. Blood dripped slowly into her arm and Dr. Thorneycroft was standing by the bed. The look he gave Nigel was close to contempt.

'She's going to be all right, thanks to quick action on the part of George Barton down at Port Roy. Your father gave permission for me to operate.' Coldly he explained the details.

'Thank you, Martin.' It was the first time Nigel had used Thorneycroft's Christian name. 'I'm sorry I was not available. I'll go and speak to my father and then I'll be back.' He made no excuses and did not see the sudden pity in Dr. Thorneycroft's eyes.

Robert offered his son no sympathy but Ann, always quick to feel for others, took his hand in hers and then kissed him.

'Don't blame yourself too much. It will all come right.'

'She didn't even tell me she was pregnant and that was my fault. I've behaved abominably. I'm sorry, Ann, I'll try to make up. I'm going back now. Do you want to see her before you go?'

'No, we'll see her in the morning. When she comes round it will be you she will want.' Ann spoke confidently.

★　　★　　★

In the morning the island was horrified by the news that Della Grant had been found stabbed to death under the trees near Boston. Her hands had been folded across her breast and there had been no attempt to hide the body. Gordon Grant said he hadn't seen her to speak to the night before but he had heard her quarrelling with a boy outside the house and had then heard her go up to her room. He had no idea she had gone out again. Did he know who the boy was? No, he hadn't an idea. Why hadn't he gone out to see?

'As a matter of fact, Inspector, I was too upset. I heard her tell the lad she was pregnant and you can guess how I felt. I decided I would talk to her this morning and find out who the man was.'

'Did anyone else hear this?'

'No, that would be impossible. The only one who sleeps in is my housekeeper and she has a room at the back of the house and she is in bed ill.'

'Thank you, Mr. Grant, you have my sympathy. It's a dreadful thing to have happened.'

Tante Marie lay on her bed with her face to the wall. Her temperature was high and she shivered as though with malaria, but when the doctor came she said she had a chill and her head hurt. She wasn't in pain at all.

Inspector Maddock did not take long to discover that Della had been seen a great deal with Paul Lacrosse until a short time ago. The boy was down at his father's warehouse and he followed the Inspector into the office, his dark face tired and unhappy.

Maddock looked at him doubtfully. He had known him from childhood and what he knew he liked.

'Did you see Della Grant last night?' Paul nodded. 'When?'

'I don't know the time. It might have been about ten or soon after.'

'Where was this?'

'Outside of her house.'

'And you quarrelled?' He shook his head. 'Then what did happen?'

'Della was angry because I was waiting for her. You see I loved her and wanted to marry her.'

So Della was the one who was angry! 'Did she tell you she was pregnant?'

Paul's face crumpled as if very close to tears. Then he nodded.

'Was it your child?'

'I don't know!' The words were wrenched from him. 'She said it wasn't. That she wouldn't be such a fool as to have a kinky-headed little nigger.'

The man looked at the drooping shoulders and downcast head. Could he have killed her because of the insult?

'What time did you get back?'

'About three this morning.'

'It had been raining for hours then. She was killed no later than midnight. The ground under her body was practically dry. Did you kill her, Paul?'

'Dear Jesus, no! I couldn't have hurt her. If I killed anyone it would have been the man who was the father of her child.'

'And who was that?'

'I don't know!'

For the first time Inspector Maddock didn't believe him. 'I think you do but I can't make you tell me but I wish you would for your own sake.'

'I tell you I don't know.'

*   *   *

When the doctor said Della was not pregnant

the Inspector was puzzled. Why had she said such a thing or did she think she was? News travels fast on a small island and it wasn't long before Nina heard that Paul Lacrosse had been questioned by the police about Miss Della's murder. She carried the news up to Tante Marie with her afternoon tea. So far she had refused anything but water. Now she sat up slowly.

'Thank you, Nina, I'll drink the tea.'

'You're feeling better.' Nina looked at her with relief. It had been a dreadful morning. Miss Della dead and Tante Marie ill. She had worked with tears pouring down her cheeks, not that she liked Miss Della but it was a dreadful thing to happen.

'Yes, I'm better. I'll get up now.'

Nina didn't argue with Tante Marie.

Tante Marie dressed slowly, lead weighted her legs and her head throbbed. Then she went to the phone. When the taxi came she was wearing her best clothes. She went first to the Church and asked for Father O'Donnell. It was a long time since she had been to confession. She knelt quietly and poured out her heart.

*   *   *

Mary was sitting on the veranda with Nigel by her side. It was Sunday afternoon two weeks later. Robert and Ann had taken the children for a picnic. The rains had stopped, the muddied streams were running clear again and already the garden was beginning to recover from the wind which had dried up the plants and scattered the leaves until it looked as if it would never bloom again. They had kept the news of Della's death from her until she was well on the mend and then she had looked at Nigel sadly.

'I'm sorry, Nigel. She was so beautiful and if I hadn't come to the island this would never have happened.'

'That's foolish, Mary. Della was steadily carving her own destruction and we were all blind except Tante Marie and perhaps her father. He didn't care and poor Tante Marie cared too much. She told Father O'Donnell the whole pitiful story. How Della's mother had found out she was Gordon Grant's mistress and Grant taunted her with the fact that she couldn't give him a son. She wanted to take Della with her but Grant refused, but before she left she made Tante Marie promise that she would care for the child. Tante Marie was incapable of handling Della although she adored her and her one hope was that she would marry a man who could do both. When she found she was trying to break up our marriage Tante Marie went quite crazy and made up her mind she must kill her. The sad thing was that she really believed Della was pregnant and it was my child.'

'And what about you, Nigel?' She had been in hospital over a week then and was well on the road to recovery but still looked fragile.

'I behaved like a fool and I've no excuses but I was never in love with Della and there was no affair.'

'I haven't any excuses, either.' She gave him a rueful smile. 'I don't know what got into me unless it was the devil in the wind. What with Tony being so difficult and that beastly morning sickness I got more and more obstinate. Every time poor Della came near I lost my sense of proportion.'

'The sickness wasn't ordinary morning sickness. That little fool, Carmen, had been dosing your fruit juice with something Della gave her. She had told her it would be good for you and whether she really believed it or whether she was terrified of Della is hard to say. It was something that old devil Papa Dan had brewed. Inspector Maddock has put the fear of the Lord in him and he'll try no more magic. Thank God it did no more than it did. There'll be no more trouble with Tony. I've talked to him. It seems that Della not only terrified him about the devil in the cave but that you were not his mother at all. The poor child was completely bewildered.' His good looking face was full of pain. 'And to think I wouldn't listen when you said she was turning him against you. Martin Thorneycroft is convinced she was a schizophrenic, poor

Tante Marie that she was utterly evil. I don't know.'

'Try to forget it, Nigel, remember her as the little girl next door. I'll be home soon and then we can talk.'

But so far there had been no talking. The children were excited to have their mother home again, Robert and Ann were bright and cheerful. Ann had temporary leave from her work until Mary was absolutely fit because she refused to leave the children in Carmen's charge in spite of the girl's protests that she would take great care of them and had meant no harm.

Mary was looking at the blue sea with its fringe of white lace breaking on the pale sand and knew that the time had come when she and Nigel must talk. He had been gentle and considerate while she had been in hospital and she believed him when he said he had never loved Della but that did not mean he loved her. He had kissed her each time he saw her but that was all. From his manner she might have been a well-loved friend and no more.

'Do you still want to go back to England, Mary? I know you had booked your passage. Ann found the tickets in your bag and cancelled them, but as soon as you are fit I'll arrange it if that is what you want.'

It was so difficult. Her heart was beating painfully. She wanted to stay, to try and pick up the threads, to get back to that blissful but all too short period when they had belonged so absolutely to each other, when she had felt love between them deep and strong, but she wasn't sure of anything now. If he had realised since then that it had never been the permanent love that makes a perfect marriage it was senseless to stay. She sat quite still, unable to find any words.

'Did you want the baby, Mary?' His voice was low.

She looked straight at him. 'Yes, Nigel, I wanted it.'

'Thorneycroft says there is no earthly reason why you should not have another later on.'

She wasn't sure if he was trying to build up something sensible or if he wanted her.

'I don't want another baby just to try and save our marriage, Nigel. I only want to stay if you want me and need me.'

'Dear Lord above, are you out of your mind? Of course I want you! If you go I've lost all I hold dear!'

'Nigel, you fool, you great big fool!' Tears filled her eyes and trickled down her cheeks. 'Why in the world didn't you say so sooner?'

'Because,' he said, going down on his knees by the side of her chair and putting his arms round her, 'I pushed you around before. I persuaded you into coming here and wouldn't take no for an answer. Now I want to be sure you want to stay.'

Her tears were suddenly mixed with laughter. She took his face in her hands and held it firmly.

'Do you think we could have a house on the hill near the hospital so that you could come in and out and where I could meet the staff more and write articles about Huahnara? Where I could learn something about your work and really feel I belong?'

'Go a bit more slowly, sweetheart.' His eyes were infinitely tender. 'All that and another baby! There is no need for you to worry about belonging.' His arms closed a little tighter. 'This is where you belong and I intend to keep you here.'

Photoset, printed and bound in Great Britain by
REDWOOD PRESS LIMITED, Melksham, Wiltshire